HARCOURT BRACE & COMPANY
1919–
1994
· SEVENTY-FIVE YEARS ·

IF I
SHOULD
DIE,
BEFORE
I WAKE

Han Nolan

IF I SHOULD DIE BEFORE I WAKE

Harcourt Brace & Company

SAN DIEGO   NEW YORK   LONDON

Requests for permission to make copies of any part of the
work should be mailed to: Permissions Department,
Harcourt Brace & Company, 6277 Sea Harbor Drive,
Orlando, Florida 32887-6777.

"Nightmarish Days," from *Lodz Ghetto*, by Alan Adelson and
Robert Lapides. Copyright © 1989 by The Jewish Heritage
Writing Project. Used by permission of Viking Penguin, a
division of Penguin Books USA Inc.

Library of Congress Cataloging-in-Publication Data
Nolan, Han.
If I should die before I wake/Han Nolan. — 1st ed.
p.   cm.
Summary: As Hilary, a Neo-Nazi initiate, lies in a coma,
she is transported to Poland at the onset of World War II,
into the life of a Jewish teenager.
ISBN 0-15-238040-X
1. Holocaust, Jewish (1939–1945) — Juvenile fiction.
[1. Holocaust, Jewish (1939–1945 — Fiction.   2. Jews —
Poland — Fiction.   3. White supremacy movements —
Fiction.]   I. Title.
PZ7.N6783If   1994
[Fic] — dc20   93-30720

Designed by G. B. D. Smith
Printed in the United States of America
First edition
A B C D E

To Brian, my husband,
and to my parents, James and Eileen Walker,
for their patience, faith, and love

And to the memory of the six million Jews
whose faces I never knew,
yet whose voices I somehow heard

IF I
SHOULD
DIE
BEFORE
I WAKE

CHAPTER ONE

Hilary

SHE'S LOOKING AT ME. She's looking at me like she knows
me. It's the arm band. She must have seen it when they carried
me in. People see my arm band and right away they think they
know me, know all about me. They don't know crap. I know
her though. I don't need any arm band to tell me about her.
It's written all over her what she is.

She's still looking at me. That's her kind, looking at me like
she knows me.

Hey, you don't know me. So don't look at me like you do.
You think with that grandmaw look you're going to undo me
and find some sweet young thing hiding behind my arm band?
What you see is what you get. It's all you get. You're just like
my mother and the Rev. and them all. Like any second I'm
going to change back into that nothing of a girl I used to be
and open my arms and say, "I love you. I love you all." Forget
it. I'm not some Barbie doll in a beauty contest. Screw it! That's
not me. Never was. That's just who they want me to be. And
why? For who? Huh?

You want to know who I am? I'm the worst possible thing
that could happen to someone like you. And if I weren't trapped
or strapped or wrapped or whatever the hell I am, I'd show
you. See, 'cause I know you. I know who you are. I can tell a
mile away. Jew lady! Yeah, I know you.

1

What you doing here anyway? You some kind of guard? You here to see I don't beat the crap outta some sick Jew? This is the Jewish hospital, isn't it? What a joke on me, huh? Having a motorcycle accident in some Hebe town and coming here to the freakin' Jew hospital. Yeah, I remember that all right. Dr. Bergensteinburger, or something, right? All of you have those look-at-me kind of names. Those so-very-Jewish names, so you can recognize each other without having to fart first.

Can't you speak or what?

Nah, you're just like all the others. Can't talk to someone like me, someone from my side of the tracks. You think you're better than me? You're nothing! Nothing! Hey, don't look at me, lady.

Yeah, now that's better.

You ever hear of us? Huh? White Power, lady! We ever come crashing against your door in the middle of the night? Maybe a rock thrown through your window? Yeah, I know, kid stuff.

We got the whole Hebe neighborhood quaking in their stinkin' stringy sideburns once though, we sure did. Redesigned their whole freakin' cemetery. By the time we got through with it, it looked like some bloody massacre took place there. Yeah, I spray painted everything in sight, so it's like, ARI—WHITE POWER—GOLDSMITH and then a big red swastika under all that Rest in Peace business they write. Yeah, bet they aren't resting in peace anymore in that stinkin' place. Made the front page of the newspaper, too. Not our local paper, that small-town crap wiper, but the freakin' *Philadelphia Inquirer!* How about that?

And that's nothing compared to what Brad and Billy H.

and Chucky B. did last night or yesterday or whenever the hell this accident happened. Hey, picture it. They dress up like Bozo the Clown, all three of them, and kidnap this Jew boy. Wrestle him to the ground in the woods back of the library. Only dumb old Simon Schulmann would be at the library till closing time on a Saturday night. He'd been there the past three Saturdays so it was practically guaranteed he'd be there again this time and taking the shortcut home through the woods, of course. Lazy Jew. See what being lazy gets you?

Always he comes out dressed in these pants that I swear don't reach down to the top of his ankles. He's got these skinny black suspenders on, too, like he's afraid his pants might slip an inch and maybe he'd look normal. Of course he always has on his little beanie cap Saturday nights, the hypocrite. He wears the thing every freakin' morning climbing on the bus, but soon as he sits his butt down and Mommy's out of sight, off it comes. If he really believes in those beanies, why the hell is he always taking his off? I'll tell you why. No balls. Jews have no balls. That's what Brad says, and he's right, too.

You know what Brad and them did with him? It's a riot, it really is. I only wish I could have been there to see old Simon's face. Girls aren't allowed to do those kinds of things in the group, but I would if I could. I would if I could. Simon's on my school bus, lives right behind me, anyway. He'd recognize me — but Brad and them, they've been out of school a couple of years already. Hey, but I'm the one who chose him as our victim. I did that all right.

So, they stuffed him in one of the big orange lockers they got in the boys' locker room at school. He's pint-sized anyway, just like all Jews. Tiny little monkeys, what they are. Tiny little crooks.

Brad said old Simon had his fists flying all over the place, like he thought he had a chance. Cut his face on the edge of the locker as they were stuffing him in.

Hey, I know what you're thinking. Poor little boy. Poor pitiful little boy. He's thirteen, okay? That's not so young. He can take it. Don't look at me with that shame-on-you look. You don't know, Grandmaw.

He's all right. Even if we are on spring break, Brad said he was screaming loud enough to wake the dead.

So what anyway. I don't care. I don't care about him or anyone except Brad.

Brad, now he knows me inside and out. He's the only one. Where is he anyway? He get hurt? Huh? You gonna talk to me, Jew lady? Look at me. Jews are always looking at the ground. Brad says it's 'cause they're always looking for pennies. Rich Jews. Rich bitch Jews. What you need to be scumming for pennies for?

I don't like the way you're looking at me. Don't pity me. Hey, don't pity me. Why do people always do that? All my life people are always pitying me. Teachers, they're the worst. They give you that simpering look and then come up and put their arm around you like they're your best buddy. They don't know me. They don't know what I'm thinking. Like when my father died. When a whole freakin' office building my father was working on collapsed and crushed him to death because his Jew boss was doing some dirty dealing with the construction, what did they know about how I felt? Nobody knew. But my teacher figures she knows all about it and she says, "Nancy dear, why don't you go sit next to poor Hilary, that's a good girl." Then when Nancy's settled next to me with her snooty nose flipped up toward the ceiling like a pop top, Mrs. Doyan adds, "Now, boys and girls, I want you all to be extra nice to our little Hilary Burke today, something very sad has happened to her father."

So of course at play period every kid in the freakin' school's asking me what happened. That's how understanding that bitch was. Yeah, she really cared.

So what anyway, right? All the hell I ever wanted was to have people leave me alone. If she had really understood, she would have at least known that about me.

So how come I can't see anything but you? Huh? Can't even see my freakin' body. Can't even move.

Know what you look like? Like some old bag lady that slept with her face pressed into the cracks of a sidewalk all night. Yeah, it's true, some gray old bag lady.

Where is everyone? Where's Brad? You can tell me that at least, can't you?

Screw it! He'll be here. He'll come. And wait till you see him. He's got eyes the color of blue ink and the biggest shoulders. Like rocks — hard, you know? I remember the first time I really got a good look at him. Yeah, I was spying on them one night down in Hack's basement. Peeking through the window. Well, hey, all that yelling I was always hearing when they'd go marching down my street, what'd you expect, right? I had to follow them, see where they were going.

So what do I see but like ten of these major hunks all with their shirts off and they're standing in a circle and one of them's got a hefty set of weights on his shoulders and the others are counting while this guy tries to lift it over his head. I recognized Hack and a couple of the others 'cause they went to my school a couple years back but this one guy — Brad — only time I'd seen him was out in front of the 7-Eleven where he once actually winked at me. Then when I started walking away, eating my stupid doughnut, I could tell he was watching me. Really, I could feel his eyes on my back.

Anyway, when they rolled the weights over to Brad he picked them up like it was marshmallows on either end of a toothpick, I swear. And he does like seventeen lifts; more than any of the other guys. When he passes it over to the next guy, Mick, I can see this boy doesn't look so hot. He picks up the weights and the others start counting and it's like, one, tuh-ew, thur-eee, fff-our. His legs are shaking like he's trying to steady an earthquake, and the weights are lopsided, one side about to conk him on the head.

He loses it after six and everyone jumps back to let the weights crash to the floor. Then it gets really weird. Mick starts backing away and all the others, without any signal, they get into this line facing him and start stalking toward him. Then Mick starts crying, swear to God, and when his back comes up against this table he turns around, pulls down his pants, and bends over. Yeah, really. And then Hack pulls out this long stringy whip thing and they each have a go at Mick with Brad being last and whipping him seventeen times. Then Mick pulls his pants back up, turns around to face the others, and wipes at his nose. He raises his right arm straight out in front of him, palm down, with his fingertips almost touching Brad's chest, and he starts shouting, "Heil, Hitler! Heil, Hitler!"

The way he said it, man, like he wasn't just five seconds ago bent over having the blood whipped out of him. He stood so tall and the others, they all together do this turn-around thing with their feet so they're facing the same way and they all raise their hands and join him, "Heil, Hitler! Heil, Hitler!" Then they put their arms on each other's shoulders and they're shouting, "Strength through unity! Power through hate! Kill

Jews! Kill Jews! Kill Jews!" And I'm there, down on my knees under a freakin' bush that smells like cat pee, trying to figure out how I'm going to manage to get up enough courage to say something clever next time I see the steamy guy with rocks for shoulders. Hey, I won't forget that night in a hurry.

Yeah, he'll come get me, all right. We stick together, us Warriors, you'll see.

Bet you he didn't even get hurt. I go flying off that motorcycle and whizzing through the air like a stone from a slingshot, and what'd I hit? Something, I know that, 'cause it felt like my whole body just shattered into a million pieces at once. I remember that, I sure do. And then snap, everything goes blank like at the end of a videotape when the movie's all over. Well, I'm here now, I'm alive — right?

Hey, where you going? Well, good riddance to you. You finally took the hint. Only a Jew would stand here like a dummy and listen to someone insult them and then look at the person like she's the one to be pitied. Only a Jew would do that. Only a dumb Jew. Hey, yeah, dumb Jew, get it. Dumb, a person who can't speak. That's you all right. Dumb Jew.

Wait a minute. Hey, come back here! What's going on? What's happening? I'm spinning!

I'm spinning backward. All around me is black. I see the old lady. Through this pinhole of light I see her. I see her face just for an instant before falling farther away, before spinning backward again, head over heels — away.

CHAPTER TWO

Hilary/Chana

WHEN I STOPPED SPINNING, I found myself walking through a sunny fall day, on a street I had never seen, in a land where I had never been, with a best friend I had never known. I was wearing a colorless wool jumper over a white blouse and itchy wool tights that sagged at my ankles. Still, I was pleased with what I was wearing. The tights were new and my best friend looked much the same as I. We even wore the same coat with the same star decorations: canary yellow stars, one on the front and one on the back. We were on our way to school, laughing and talking in a language I did not know, yet I understood.

As we approached the next street, we stopped laughing. I felt my shoulders stiffen and my throat go dry as I took hold of my friend's hand and we timidly set foot down the street. There were other children on the road, laughing and pushing at each other as we had done earlier. They weren't afraid, and I suddenly knew that it had something to do with our stars. I knew, too, that we were taking a great chance going to school, and as we walked, we scanned the streets left and right. I did not know what we were searching for until they were in front of me, two men in uniforms with guns in their hands. Without thinking, both of us hopped off the sidewalk. That was the rule. When these men in their uniforms were on the sidewalk, we had to get off or they'd shoot us. We expected them to turn us away, saying we were no longer allowed to attend school with the other students. Instead, they led us to a building that on the outside smelled like manure and on the inside like disinfectant. There were several women there, like us, with yellow stars stitched to their clothing. They were down on their knees with guards behind them, and the guards were laughing, mocking them while they scrubbed the floors, some with their hands and some with a kind of cloth.

One of the men shouted at us. The shout was so loud and it frightened me so, I didn't hear what he said. He slapped me in the face.

"Tights off!" he repeated in a language that so repulsed me to hear I wanted to scream, but I didn't. I knew he'd only slap me again, or worse.

I kicked off my shoes and tried to scramble out of my tights, but I wasn't fast enough and the guard kicked me in the back. It wasn't hard and it didn't hurt, but my feet were still in the tights. I lost my balance and fell onto the floor and into the disinfectant. The men behind me laughed, but no one scrubbing the floor laughed, or even looked up.

"She's just a young girl," I heard someone say, someone down there on the floor, close to me. I wiped the wet slop off my coat and stood up. The others kept scrubbing.

I was led away from my friend, down the hall to the other end, where a woman was scrubbing the stairs.

"You work with her, clumsy Jew!" The officer spit. "Use those to scrub." He pointed at my tights.

I dropped to my knees and dunked my tights into the bucket beside me. I didn't look up and I didn't speak to the woman who worked on the stairs with me. I just dunked and scrubbed, dunked and scrubbed. It must have been a half hour before I took a chance and looked around. It was then that I noticed that the woman beside me was my neighbor and my mother's best friend, Estera Hurwitz. I wanted to sing with joy when I saw her. I inched over closer to her and as we scrubbed we knocked elbows. I saw her smile, but she didn't look up. Still I knew she knew it was I who was beside her, and the occasional knocking of our elbows gave both of us courage, a reminder that we weren't alone.

I watched the circular movements of her hands and tried to copy the rhythm. Her movements were even and strong, strong like her hands, used to hard labor but not to such humiliation. She dunked her rag into the bucket, wrung it out, and spread it back on the stairs. It was then that I saw for the first time what she had in her hand, what so many of the other women had in their hands — her own underpants. I wanted to cry out, to weep for these women, and I wanted to kill the men, the officers who were doing this to us. I scrubbed harder, faster, trying not to think about it, trying not to cry. I wanted to be strong like Estera Hurwitz, like my own mother, both of them so brave, so strong. Yes, I had to be like my mother — my mother! Was she here? Please, dear God, not my mother. I could not bear it. I inched closer to my mother's best friend and asked in a voice so low that even I could hardly hear it, "My mother? Here?"

Mrs. Hurwitz kept scrubbing and I wasn't sure she heard. I was about to repeat my question when I saw her nod.

A sound slipped through my lips before I could catch myself. Within seconds I had an officer behind me, the barrel of his gun thrust against my shoulder. I kept scrubbing, acting as if it wasn't there. What did I care if I was shot? It would be better than seeing my mother, so beautiful, so proud, at the feet of these men, scrubbing their floors with her underpants. Let them shoot me, I thought.

He stood like that for only a minute and then left, swearing at me, the clumsy Jew, as he walked away. The sound of his voice made me sick. The sound of his shiny black boots, reminding me of the victorious march down the center of our streets not long ago, made me want to spit in his face. Oh, if I could only spit in his face. I felt tears running down my own face, and I let them drop onto the stairs. I rubbed them in — hard, as hard as I could. Then I decided, no, I would not wash these steps with my tears but with my spit — my contempt. And so together, the rest of that morning and into the afternoon, with each clank of our bucket, Estera Hurwitz and I spit at the men with the guns and the shiny black boots.

Finally, late in the afternoon, they allowed us to leave. My legs could hardly straighten as I pulled myself up, using the banister for support. My knees looked like two red doorknobs, round and swollen. Mrs. Hurwitz was even worse, and I had to help her as she hobbled down the stairs. I led her out into the wonderful fresh air, and the two of us just stood and inhaled. Even manure smelled good after breathing cleaning fumes all day.

The other women had already left, and so together, Mrs. Hurwitz and I set off, eager to rejoin our families.

We had been walking for a quarter of an hour when we saw a bit of commotion farther down the street.

"Come on" — Mrs. Hurwitz tugged at my coat sleeve — "I know another way."

I was just about to follow her when two officers shifted their position and I glimpsed between them, dangling from a tree by his coat, my father.

"No!" I shouted, and I ran down the sidewalk, forgetting the sidewalk rule.

Three officers turned and aimed their guns at me.

I heard my father shout, "Go home, Chana!"

I ignored him. How dare these beasts do this to him! Didn't they know who he was?

"That's my father, let him go!" I pointed at him and demanded again, "Let him go!"

The men began to laugh. It was such a big joke. Then they turned and aimed their guns at my father.

"No!" I shouted again, speaking to them in their own language. "Why are you doing this?"

One man spoke, without looking at me, without taking his eyes off of my father — my dear, dear tata.

"Your lazy, filthy father refuses to work. He's too tired, he says. He needs to rest, he says, and so he leans against this tree. Ha! He needs this tree to hold him up. You see, we've helped him. Now he can rest."

The blood was rushing to my head so fast I thought it might explode. How dare they treat my father like this, and how dare all these people — for I had suddenly noticed there were many neighbors of ours — how dare they stand there watching and laughing, no one bothering to help.

I moved closer, ignoring my father as he tried to shoo me away with his hands. "My father is ill," I said. "He has a heart condition. Please let him down. I'll do his work for him. What is it you want him to do?"

This, too, was funny to these men, but one of them led me behind a long building to another street. There were many men already there, all friends of my father's, shoveling dirt and heaping it up into a pile against the building. The officer pointed his gun at my father's shovel. "You work," he said, "and don't rest, or you, too, will hang in the tree."

I grabbed the shovel and began my work with gusto, following behind a young boy about my age. I scooped up the dirt and pitched it against the building. I tried to ignore the jeering on the other side. I would work until the job was done. Then Tata and I could leave, and he and I would never speak of this day to anyone, ever.

My pile of dirt was rising clear up to the level of the first window and yet I wasn't tired. Tata, he would be proud of me. I smiled to myself and then caught a glimpse of someone, a girl, staring back at me through the window. She had a face like mine only older, wiser looking, especially the eyes. They were dark and deep set and looked at me as if they knew everything about me, about the world. I could see pain in those eyes. They were trying to tell me something. I stopped shoveling, only for a second, only to understand. Then I heard two shots explode on the other side of the building.

"Tata!" I cried. I dropped the shovel and fell into the dirt pile screaming, knowing somehow that from that day forward, I would be screaming forever.

CHAPTER THREE

Hilary/Chana

I CAN HEAR MYSELF screaming but it doesn't sound like me. It's not my voice. I stop. It scares me to be screaming with someone else's voice.

Old Grandmaw's staring at me again, like we've been here all the time, just looking at one another. I want to roll away from her or close my eyes, anything to get away from her, but I can't move. She floats toward me, like some kind of spirit, with a wet cloth in her hand. She wipes my face, and then I hear her dunking the cloth. I hear the water running off it as she lifts it up again, and I think of me and Estera Hurwitz, dunking our undergarments into our bucket.

I don't feel so good. Hey, Grandmaw, get me that Dr. Hamburgerstein, or a nurse or something.

Don't look at me. And don't think I'm crying over you, Jew lady. What's wrong with you anyway? Your hair's all mashed flat in the back. Why do you always look as if you just got out of bed?

Well, I don't feel sorry for you, whatever your problem is, and I'll tell you something else just so you know, no freakin' dream's going to change my thinking. That's all it was. Stupid dream.

Do you know about it? You look as if you do. You look

as if you know everything. Jews always think they know everything.

My father died. They hung him in a tree and shot him. I mean I dreamed my father died. I mean, this other father died, not *my* father. Not my *real* father. My real father died when I was five. Roy Burke was his name. Just so you know. Just so you know I'm not crying 'cause of some frickin' frackin' dream. And cool it with the cloth already. Wipe your own face. What do you care about me anyway?

Making me scrub floors with a pair of tights. I can tell you that'd never happen in real life. No one controls me like that. No one.

What's that? Hear that? That's my mother. I can pick her tippy-tappy footsteps out anytime.

Yeah, hear that? Those are her bracelets. She must have a hundred of those cheap pieces of tin clanking around her arms. Oh, and she's got this big old zircon ring. If she touches you with that thing on, watch out. Her rings are always too big for her fingers so they slip around to the palm of her hand, and then she like taps you on the shoulder or something and you're freakin' bruised for life.

"Hilary? Baby?"

Hey, Grandmaw, get her out of here. I mean it. I don't want to speak to her. You know she'll blame this whole accident on Brad.

"It's so quiet in here, just you and that other patient there, both of you barely breathing. And all those bandages and tubes, just look at you. Baby, can you hear me?"

Grandmaw? Why can't I see her? Why do I see only you?

"Your face, your beautiful face. Will those bruises go away? You always had the most beautiful complexion. No acne, rosy cheeks, ruby lips, silky blond hair — before you shaved it all off, that is. You were just like Alice in Wonderland, remember?

"Couldn't they wipe off that blood?

"Baby, can you hear me? I'm here. Right by your side."

So what's she want, a freakin' standing ovation? It's all show, this coming to see me. She doesn't care.

"I brought you something. It's a book. Well, it's my Bible. You can't exactly read it yet, I know, but I can read it to you."

See. This is her way of torturing me. Like I want to hear her quoting Scripture. That's all show, too, her church and Bible thing.

"That awful Brad boy asked for you. I tell you that because I'm a good Christian woman and I won't tell you any lies or keep anything from you, but that boy's got nerve. Won't come in here himself. No, not into a Jewish hospital. Shows how important he thinks you are. No guts. That's what it is. Sure, it's easy to hide behind bushes and attack people in the dark, but we won't see him anywhere around here, I tell you."

Hide behind bushes? What does she know?

"Figures, he escapes the accident with hardly a scratch and here you are lying on death's dark doorstep.

"It's God's will, I suppose.

"I'd just like to know how this accident happened. Of course Brad was most likely drunk. Takes after his drunken father, that boy does, and he'll be just as violent with his own family, too, mark my words."

Shows what you know. And like you're the perfect parent? At least his father's always there. His father didn't run away and leave Brad all alone for three freakin' days when he was only five freakin' years old. And anyway, he didn't have anything to drink that night. It was too important a night for drinking.

16

After the kidnapping Billy and Chucky drop him off at his house and he gets on his bike and picks me up. Just like he said he would, out in front of the 7-Eleven. Rides up on his Harley, his white teeth shining out of the dark, and I know right away it went okay. And we're laughing at each other, just happy, you know? I hop on and hug him around his waist and we go tearing outta there over to Chucky's.

When we pull up outside of Chucky's house and Brad turns off the motor, I can hear the shouting coming from the basement. Brad grabs my hand and we charge into the house. The shouting's louder now, and it's like that first night when I joined the Warriors, 'cause they're going to initiate another girl into the group and everyone's real hyped. We go down into the basement lit up with red light bulbs and black candles, and there's everyone with their robes on and facing the poster on the wall. We slip into our robes, blood red with these black patches on the shoulders that show swords bent into the shape of swastikas. We find our places in line and join them.

"Heil, Hitler! Heil, Hitler!" we shout.

Hitler's face stares back at us, larger than life, just like the man himself. We just keep shouting, and I can feel the goose bumps crawling all over me as I feel the excitement, the unity, the thunder in the room. There's like twenty of us there, and we don't stop shouting until the Great Warrior arrives, and by then my voice is so hoarse I'm not even sure I'm making any noise. When Hack makes his way up to the front of the room, we sit down and the ceremony begins.

Meg O'Toole is called up to the front and is handed two unlit candles, one for each hand. Brad goes up, rolls out the Nazi flag, and drapes it around her waist, tucking it in so it stays up. Then Hack commands the rest of us to stand and form a circle. The room's real quiet when we do this, no shoving and giggling. Then Hack unrolls the female initiation scroll and begins.

"Do you, Megan Reese O'Toole, promise to uphold the principles of white supremacy and the purity of white womanhood?"

"I do!" she shouts through strands of yellow hair hanging in her face.

"Do you take the Aryan race to be your one and only religion?"

"I do!"

"Do you recognize all Jews as children of Satan?"

"I do!"

"Do you promise to do your part in bringing about the Final Solution — the destruction of all Jews and the creation of a united Aryan nation?"

"I do!"

"Do you acknowledge that you are a seed bearer and life giver of the white race, and in so being you will do no race mixing, upon pain of death?"

"I do!"

"Do you acknowledge yourself to be a woman, and there-fore the weaker vessel and servant to the one man given to you in marriage?"

She looks over at her boyfriend, just like I did with Brad during my ceremony, and shouts, "I do!"

"Do you swear to uphold the secrecy of these meetings and the activities of the Aryan Warriors?"

"I do!"

"Megan Reese O'Toole, your ultimate role will be that of wife — serving your husband — and of mother, giving birth to our future. By accepting this role in the race wars, you will achieve a place in history. No higher honor can be so bestowed upon a woman.

"As a member of this den, you may attend and participate in all general meetings. You may wear the arm band and the robe on such occasions as is necessary. Participation in 'outings' is at the discretion of the Great Warrior."

Then Hack lifts his head up from the scroll and nods to Chucky. Chucky steps forward, pulls out his plastic lighter, and lights Meg's candles. Meg steps forward and we pull back so she can walk through the circle and over to the table where a cross made out of two broken branches tied together with a strand of rawhide stands in a pewter mug.

She lights one branch with the red candle and we all say, "The blood of all Jews shall burn." Then she lights the other branch and we say, "Their ashes shall become crusts in hell."

Then she sets the candles in the holders placed on either side of the burning cross and turns to face us.

Hack raises his right hand out in front of him and shouts, "Sister! Heil, Hitler!"

"Heil, Hitler!" the rest of us shout, including Meg. Then we all step up to the table and pass around this sharp pocket-knife. We cut a slit in our palms and squeeze out the blood. Then we go back to our circle with Meg in the center and she goes up to each of us, one at a time, and presses her bloody palm to ours and we say, "Sister, welcome," and she says "Brother" or "Sister" back. Then when she's gone all the way around, Brad removes the flag and Hack hands her her robe.

After she puts it on and joins our circle, Hack says to her, "You are a member of the Great Aryan Warriors. This is now your family. You belong to us and we to you. As long as you follow the laws of this den, we will protect you. Heil, Hitler!"

I can't help it, I'm standing there crying just like I did during my own ceremony, but then as our shouts get louder and stronger, I can feel the atmosphere change and it's like a party, everyone standing close and proud.

Then we start chomping on chips and M&M's and telling each other about our victories that night, laughing and shouting and carrying on. And then at the end, we're shouting "White Power" and "Death to Jews" and more "Heil, Hitlers," and you never felt such power. Like we owned the world. We owned it. I swear we held it in the palms of our hands and it was up to us whether we were going to crush it or hold it up.

That's our power, Mother. We're together, united and strong, like a real family.

Yeah, being in that room, with all the shouting and the ceremony and having Brad's arm around me, I knew I'd die for any one of them if I had to. I'd die for the cause. I could tell, too, just by looking at all the faces, the shining eyes, that everyone felt like that. That's our power. We didn't need to drink. We were drunk with our own victories, our power.

So get it straight, Mother, it wasn't any drinking that caused the accident. It was the stinkin' rain. By the time we left the meeting and made our way over to Burleigh it was pouring and we took a skid going around Bishop's corner. Brad's good on a bike, Mother; he couldn't help the rain. Anyway, he wasn't drunk.

"I just pray to God that you had nothing to do with the disappearance of that little Schulmann boy. It's all over the papers."

He's still missing? Brad said he was screaming loud enough to wake the dead. How long have I been here? Hey, Grandmaw, how long I been in here? Well, it can't be too long. It just seems like forever 'cause I can't move, right?

Now don't go giving me that suffering-cow look again. Look at me. Mother says I'm on death's dark doorstep and you know what? I feel like death, so don't be giving me that suffering look. Jews always think they've got a monopoly on suffering or something. Hey, I know suffering. I don't need to be a part of someone else's. They'll find the stupid kid. Besides, how bad could it be being shut up in one of those big old lockers? How bad could it be? So it's a little dark. And hot I guess, or maybe it's cold. Do they leave the heat on over vacation? The kid's probably out by now anyway, right? While Mother's been giving me her phony see-how-much-I-care speech, the police have been rescuing Simon. Right?

I guess if he's got to go to the bathroom he'll just do it in his pants. Well, so what, right? Worse could happen. He can breathe. The locker's got vents. Who the hell cares about him anyway? Jew boy. Who the hell cares?

"I won't disturb the others if I read to you, will I? I'll just read to you quietly.

"I suppose I can use this chair. Now let's see . . .

"God is our refuge and strength,
a very present help in trouble.
Therefore we will not fear though the earth should change,
though the mountains shake in the heart of the sea;
though its waters roar and foam,
though the mountains tremble with its tumult."

Grandmaw? Hey! It's happening again. You can stop it, I know you can.

I'm falling back into that dark place, spinning away,

spinning down. I can see the darkness and the pinpoint of light where the old lady's face stares out at me. The pinpoint begins to grow, letting in more light, shutting out the darkness, erasing Grandmaw's face and bringing into focus a room, square and small.

CHAPTER FOUR

Chana

THE SIGHTS AND SOUNDS before me were instantly clearer than the last time I had visited this other world. The colors, the images, were sharper. As I looked about the room, with its high ceiling and creamy white walls, empty fireplace, and furniture in shades of blue and brown worn into comfort, I knew immediately who, and where, I was. I knew this time that I was thirteen years old, living in Poland, and that this was my living room. The people gathered there with me were my family. I knew, too, that we were still "sitting *shiva*," in mourning, for my father. The two plain mirrors facing one another on opposite walls were covered with white cloths, and I understood, as if I had always known, that this was part of the ritual of the *shiva*. The circle of low stools upon which my mother and Bubbe, my grandmother, and Zayde, my grandfather, sat were also part of this seven-day ritual of mourning my father.

The room was cold, or perhaps it was just I who was cold, sitting on the bare wooden floor next to my mother's stool. I tucked my legs and feet up under my dress and huddled in closer to Mama. I wanted her to pat my head, thinking her touch, her love, would warm me, but she was not thinking about me.

I was aware of the peace, the dead quiet in the room, the way one is aware of it after a loud, long, crashing clamor has ended. There is usually that sense of relief; the body relaxes and one continues with what one was doing before the noise began. This time, however, was different. I remained tense. My muscles ached with readiness, my eyes were tired of the ever alert, almost unblinking vigilance I kept over the house, the family, myself. Yes, there was peace, but what came before it, and what was sure to come again, made that peace hover over the room like the blade of a guillotine. I tried to calm my nerves by reading to my six-year-old sister, Anya, who sat beside me, restlessly playing with Nadzia, the baby of the family.

"Sit still, Anya," I reprimanded. "You are missing the most interesting part. *Shiva* is almost over, you can be still for just a few more hours."

"I know, but I cannot wait to get some fresh air. Can you, Chana? Can you not wait?"

I looked toward the window by the piano. The curtains were closed, but I had peered out earlier and knew what the weather was like.

"It is too cold and gray outside. Even when the rabbi comes I do not think I will want to go out."

"It is not the cold you are afraid of, it is the Germans." Anya turned to Mama. "Will the Germans come to get us when we go outside, like Jakub said?"

"Hush, Anya!" Mama said. "No more talk of the Germans. Your brother has filled your head with too many horror stories."

"But Tata—his story is true. What Chana said was true. They shot Tata, hanging from the tree."

"Hush, Anya," Mama whispered.

Zayde looked up from his lap. "Jakub is wrong, Anya. His mind is so full of killings and burnings it has got him running this way and that, and he goes nowhere. He should be here with his family. It is a disgrace to us all and to your father that he is not here sitting *shiva*."

I watched as Zayde's face grew redder and redder, his head again bent low over his lap. He was like my father that way. We always knew how angry Tata was by the shades of red his face turned. Looking at Zayde now, I knew he was very angry indeed. I tried to change the subject, but before I could get two words out, my brother walked through the door.

"Bad news," Jakub said as he hung his hat and coat up on the rack by the door. He turned to face Zayde, the now-familiar challenge in his eyes.

"We must pack our things, only what we need most, and be ready by six o'clock tonight."

Zayde stood up and stretched. "This nonsense again, Jakub. And where is it now we are going?"

"Nonsense is it? Only four blocks down, the houses are empty. Not a person is left. The Germans have taken them!"

Zayde's eyes darted about the room. Mama stood up and collected Nadzia up off the floor and held her close to her face.

"God, grant that they come here in time," she whispered as she began rocking the baby in her arms.

"Who, Mama? The Germans?" Anya asked, alarm sounding in her voice.

I grabbed Anya's arm. "No, silly, the people who are coming to take Nadzia away. They are coming today, remember?"

Anya jumped up off the floor and threw her arms around Mama's legs. "Why are they only taking Nadzia? Do I not need protection from the Germans, too?"

Mama patted Anya's head. "Of course you do, and I will protect you. When Nadzia is gone . . ." Mama paused and closed her eyes. "When Nadzia is gone, I will be able to pay extra attention to you and make sure nothing and no one ever hurts you."

"You promise, Mama? Truly, truly promise?"

"Of course I do."

Anya buried her head in Mama's dress and began sobbing. "Oh, Mama, poor Tata. Poor, poor Tata. How could it be he is not with us?"

Bubbe, who had been silent and still through most of these seven days, called Anya to her.

She held both of Anya's hands in hers and spoke in a firm, knowing voice. "He *is* with us, Anya, as God is with us."

Anya stepped back from Bubbe. "Then he is *not* with us, because God is not with us. He would not let this happen. He would not take Tata right when we need him most."

"Anya, please! Is anyone going to listen to me?" Jakub looked around the room at each of us. He was only fifteen years old and yet the weight of the world seemed to bear down on his shoulders so hard I thought it would surely crush him. His eyes, once the color of the black mud his shoes carried in each day, had a gray cast to them now. It was as though the cold gray clouds outside had settled there for good, no longer allowing him to see the sun.

I wanted to cry for him, or for Tata, or maybe just for myself. I felt as Anya had; God was not there with us. Tata was gone, completely gone, as though he had never existed. Bubbe had said that our memories of him would keep him near, but we had no time for memories.

Although we kept within our home, there had been little solitude; Jakub had seen to that. On the very day of Father's burial, during the *seudat havra'ah*, the meal that is served after the funeral, Jakub, already late, rushed in with panic in his eyes and voice. He told us that we all must pack our things and run.

"If we do not leave now, right away, those Nazis will send us to the German work camps. They'll make us dig more of their infernal ditches and build roads that will help them win their war, beating us all the while, I am sure. If we go to the Russian zone we will be safe," he said, still panting with panic.

I could see the fury in Mama's eyes. In front of all her closest friends, her oldest child had refused to go to his own father's funeral. Instead he was scurrying from house to house, collecting news, adding to the hysteria that was spreading through every street and alley.

It was Zayde who spoke to him, on that first day of *shiva*, trying to steady his voice. "Now, you will listen to me. We will not have such craziness brought into this house. Respect this day of mourning, Jakub, and understand that we are going to continue with our lives in spite of the war, and the Nazis. And right now that means sitting *shiva* and honoring and mourning the man who gave you this life you are struggling so hard to protect."

"But, Zayde, I am honoring Tata by asking you all to do what he would have wanted. He would not stay where they do not allow him to have a business or even to walk down the street without fearing for his life. Every day people are disappearing. They are dragged off the streets to do some menial task and then they are beaten or — or killed. He would not stay where there is so little food, where there is no chance for dignity."

"And across the River Bug, where Russia occupies Poland, if we ever made it there without them shooting us first, you think life would be better? It is wartime, son. Food will be scarce everywhere, and who will give us jobs? The jobs, they will go to the Russians. We have no place to go, and no money to get us there. We have no choice, we must stay here and wait." Zayde stepped closer to Jakub. "It's not safe for us anywhere, but we must not fear, such insanity cannot last. You will see, evil always destroys itself. We will pray, Jakub, and have faith in God, in our deliverance. All the hysteria will soon die down, it has to." Zayde put his arm around Jakub's shoulder and guided him toward the table.

Mr. Hurwitz, who was standing beside Mama, smiled and held his hand out to Jakub. "It is all difficult and frightening, but we are all together and —"

"No!" Jakub shouted and broke away from Zayde. "I cannot afford to be a *luftmensh*, walking around with my head in the clouds. None of us can. Look around you. Do you not see what is happening out there? They killed Tata, remember? He was shot for no reason by those — those — Nazis. And the *shul*, our beautiful synagogue, they set it on fire. It is just ashes now. And neighbors" — Jakub sobbed in hurt and frustration — "neighbors who were once our friends are suddenly spitting on us and laughing at us. They kick us and beat us and — and I will not stay here and *wait!* I will not wait to be murdered. I am leaving. I shall join up with the partisans in the forest and fight the Nazis." He ran toward his room and then turned back to face Mr. Hurwitz. "And Mosze is coming with me; he is next door packing right now."

During the next two days the air was thick with panic, the guillotine hovering ever closer. Closed off as we were from all the news except what Jakub and our friends could bring inside, we were unable to sift out the truth from the rumor. Sadly, Tata was all but forgotten. Good friends rushed in uttering the short prayer, "May the Almighty comfort you among the mourners for Zion and Jerusalem," and then Tata and his memory were abruptly dismissed. It was on to the latest news, the latest information on the laws set down by the Nazis to make life for Jews more impossible. Even Zayde could no longer demand that Jakub remain with us. No one could say which was the safer path. Was it wiser to try to escape without travel permits, the Stars of David torn from all clothing — meaning certain imprisonment or even death if one were caught? Or was it better to remain there at home while rumors of Jews being dragged out to the woods to dig their own graves before being shot became facts, as the list of friends and neighbors who had disappeared grew longer?

Only Bubbe remained calm, living in a world of certainty as she did. Not only did she have a sixth sense about things, bringing people from near and far to seek her advice, but she had total faith in God. Somehow she was able to see a much larger picture of life and humanity than most people. It was this constant faith, and her calm, Mama said, that kept Bubbe looking so young and gave her so much energy. I tried to imitate her when, on the second night of *shiva*, we said good-bye to Jakub and Mosze. We watched them walk away into the shadows, away into the night, until as far as we could see, they were the night.

On the outside I felt sure I looked like Bubbe — that same hint of sadness in my eyes, acceptance and faith in my posture, standing straight and tall — but inside, I felt as if a giant rat were gnawing away at my stomach.

As Zayde closed the door behind the boys, Mama fell to the floor and cried. I forgot about wanting to be like Bubbe and started to run to Mama, to comfort her the way we had done during the day of the funeral, but Bubbe held me to her and whispered, "Leave her, Chana."

It was hard to watch my mother in so much pain. I wanted to be there with her, to cry with her, but I couldn't. I was saving my tears for Tata. I was storing them up for when *shiva* was over and I could play my violin, and remember. While I played, I could imagine us together again. He would be at the piano, his long fingers stretching like wings across the keys, and I would stand beside him with my violin. Together we would play the music of our favorite composers: Bach and Mozart.

I left Bubbe's side and moved over to the violin, which sat upon the piano bench. I closed my eyes and ran my hand along its worn leather case, and leaving the Germans and Jakub and Mama far behind, I dreamed of the last time Tata and I had played together.

Three long days after Jakub had fled toward Russia, he returned, dirty, thinner, and defeated. Saying nothing, he brushed past all our open arms and retreated to his bedroom. A moment later Mr. and Mrs. Hurwitz entered our home with such a look of horror and disbelief on their faces we knew immediately what had happened. Jakub had stopped by their house before coming home, to tell them the story of their son's death.

He had died because of a loaf of bread. It was as simple and as horrible as that. Neither my brother nor Mosze had the proper papers necessary to cross the country legally and so, like so many others, they planned to travel through the woods at night toward the River Bug — the dividing line between German- and Russian-occupied Poland — and sleep under cover as best as they could during the day. On the morning of the second day, Mosze must have felt the knapsack he was sleeping on slip out from beneath his head. He looked up to find an old man squatting on the ground and rifling through the sack. A moment later the man located the bread, pulled it out, and fled. From his cover of leaves and dirt, Jakub had watched all this, too, and it took both boys a moment to realize that what had happened had not been a dream. Without thinking, Mosze jumped up and took off after the old man. Jakub called after him, but Mosze ignored him and a minute later the old man and he were standing beneath the morning sun, fighting over the loaf of bread. Jakub stood up and had just decided to go and help his friend when he heard the gunshots. He turned and spotted four Nazis standing in a row a few yards away from his friend and the old man, their rifles held high as they waited for their bullets to hit their marks. Jakub ducked back behind the brush and watched as Mosze and the old man fell, one on top of the other, the loaf of bread squashed beneath them both.

Yes, it was Jakub who had kept things in a constant turmoil, preventing us from mourning Tata properly, and here he was again, on the seventh and last day of sitting *shiva*, telling us to pack up our things. Had he not learned anything? Had our father's and his best friend's deaths not shown him anything? I resented the way he kept trying to take Tata's place, telling us all what to do, trying to erase the last bits of Tata's memory we might carry.

Without thinking, I found myself jumping up off the floor, tears streaming down my face, and hurling myself at Jakub. I knocked him down and sat on his stomach and began pounding his arms and chest.

"Why should we listen to you?" I screamed. "Why? Who do you think you are anyway? It is all your fault! All of it! I hate you, you are worse than any Germans. To them Tata was a stranger, a nobody, but to you? Was he a nobody to you, too? You have taken Tata away. You will not even let us mourn. You with all your bad news!"

Zayde was struggling to pull me off Jakub, but I had grabbed my brother around the waist with my legs and would not let go. I was still hurling my hateful words at Jakub when there was a knock on the door. We all stopped, frozen in our places. Was this the guillotine falling at last, quick, sharp, final? During *shiva* no one knocked, a visitor just entered the home, perhaps with food to share and a kind word or two. Jakub was the first to react as another set of knocks pounded on the door. He sat up, shoving me aside as though I were a mere blanket covering his chest.

"Let us not be foolish," he said. "No Germans would politely knock on our door."

CHAPTER FIVE

Chana

JAKUB WAS RIGHT. No German would be waiting patiently behind the door while we mustered up the courage to answer it. However, it had not been that long ago, before Tata was killed, when they had charged through our house, seizing our radio and two of our best quilts and ordering Tata and Zayde to report to them for work the next day with shovels in their hands. For me that had been the beginning of all the craziness, and now I could not trust anything—even something as innocent as a knock on the door.

I looked over at Bubbe. We all did. She always knew who was at the door. It was one of her "gifts," as she called them. Her expression was one of pleasure, as though she were expecting to see an old friend on the other side, and Mama, noting her expression, rushed forward and threw open the door.

"You're here! You've made it!" Mama cried as she threw her free arm around a woman's neck and then kissed her on both cheeks. "And Oskar, you, too." She hugged him. "You've worked a miracle. Please, please come in. You are safe?"

"There was no problem, but please we are Helga and Fritz now and this is our precious daughter, Gerta." He took Nadzia from Mama's arms and examined her face and fingered her hair. "She will pass, of course. There's no need to worry."

Anya stepped forward. "She will pass, Mama? What does

that mean, and why are Oskar and Roza calling her Gerta? Isn't Nadzia going to England? Where are your American friends? I thought you said those people you taught Polish to, those Americans, remember, they were supposed to keep Nadzia."

Roza laughed. "So many questions, Anya. You must be a very smart girl."

Anya was not to be sidetracked. "What does it mean, she will pass?" she asked again.

"She doesn't look Jewish," Jakub spit out. "Her eyes are blue and her hair, what little she has, is blond. She could pass for German like Oskar and Roza." He eyed them with disgust. "How does it feel to suck up to those — those — "

"That's enough!" Zayde stepped forward, his face a deep purple. "Oskar and Roza have risked their lives to come here, and they will be risking it again as they cross the borders with their false passports. It's because of people like them that so many have been able to escape."

"Yes, people who can *pass*, but we, we are not fair enough so we are to suffer, we are to be beaten up and torn out of our houses and sent who knows where. And for what? What sin have we committed?"

"Those are not their rules, Jakub. You cannot blame what the Germans have done on Oskar and Roza," Bubbe said as she stepped forward with a large leather-bound book in her hands. "They are giving little Nadzia a chance."

"It's all right, we understand," Oskar said as he stepped farther into the room. He looked sadly at Jakub, his arms still cradling Nadzia. "It is not fair, but it is life, and we each have to decide the best way to live it, despite the circumstances." He turned to face the rest of us and said, "But where is Icek? He is not sick with the heart again, I hope?"

"He is dead, Oskar. Chana found him. The Germans, of course," Mama said.

"*Baruch дayan emet,*" whispered Oskar and Roza together. "Blessed be the one true Judge."

We all stood silently and let the words live among us, a salve for our own sick hearts.

Bubbe broke the silence at last. "Please, you don't have much time before your train; tell us about our friends in England. They are well?"

"Yes," said Roza. "We'll need to be going soon, but they are very well indeed and look forward to having little Nadzia join them. They've turned their spare bedroom into a sunny little nursery. But you haven't changed your mind, have you?" she asked, glancing at Mama's uneasy expression.

Mama smiled, but I saw the tears welling in her eyes. "No, she'll be safer with them," she replied. "They'll treat her as if she were their own, I know. Please give them our love and our deepest gratitude."

Roza returned the smile. "You were so good to them while they lived here; they're just happy to be returning the favor."

"I did so little, and they paid me for the Polish lessons. Really, I fear it is too much to ask."

"Nonsense." Oskar handed Nadzia back to Mama. Mama drew her up to her face, and then squeezed her in her arms.

"You did more than give them lessons," said Oskar. "You were their friend and their guide, and this will not be for long—surely such a war as this cannot last."

As I stood there in our living room, listening to this couple speak in a mixture of Polish and Yiddish, watching everyone smiling and hovering around Nadzia, I felt the floor beneath me begin to tilt as though I were on board a ship. For the first time, all that was happening to us, had been happening to us, struck me like a rock hurled at my chest, crushing my sternum, taking my breath away. I moved unsteadily and unnoticed toward Mama's stool and sat down. It was all, suddenly, too much for me to take in. Nadzia was leaving, and Tata was dead. Jakub and Mosze had tried to escape to Russia, and Jakub came back alone. And four blocks away the Germans had driven out the families living there and had taken them—where? Jakub had never said where. To the labor camps? Where were *we* going? What would happen to us? Would we ever see Nadzia again? I couldn't stand not knowing.

My hands trembled as Mama called me forward to say goodbye to my dear baby sister. I took her in my quivering arms and hugged and kissed her good-bye. I was determined not to cry. My first tears were to be for Tata, and they had to wait until after the *shiva,* when I could play my violin. That was my rule; and in this crazy, frightening time, that rule became the only thing that kept me from walking the streets, screaming and raging against all that had happened.

I stood back and watched Bubbe hand over the leather-bound photo album.

"So our Nadzia will know us always," Bubbe said. "There are letters inside from each of us, and instructions for you, and pictures with our names written below them. She will need to know."

She will need to know. Bubbe had said it with such meaning, such purpose, that I was struck again with so much fear I didn't think I could remain standing.

"We'll take good care of your precious Nadzia, you can be sure," said Roza. "I only wish you could all come with us."

I couldn't listen to any more. I gave Nadzia one last squeeze and hurried away into my bedroom, the bedroom I had shared with Anya and Nadzia. I had hated sharing it. I had hated listening to the baby crying and screaming half the night until Mama or Tata would drag in and remove her. And now, I prayed that I would be given a chance someday to share my room again with my littlest sister. I fell upon my bed and prayed for emptiness. I didn't want to think, or feel, or hurt anymore. I just wanted to lie there, numb, until it was all over. Until Tata and Mosze and Nadzia could come back. Until we could all dress up in our finest clothes, light the candles, bless the wine and the bread, and sit down together with our friends for the Shabbos.

There was a knock on the door and Bubbe came in.

"They have left, Chana."

I rolled away from her and faced the wall. "Good."

"Yes. Good for Nadzia, but maybe not for Chana?"

I rolled back over. "What did you mean, Bubbe, when you said, 'She will need to know'? Remember? When you handed them the album?"

"I remember, yes." Bubbe sat down on the edge of my bed.

I sat up. "What do you know? What do you see? You see something, you do."

"No, I cannot see clearly, but I know Nadzia will need to know about her family and where she came from. That is always important, to have a history, a background."

"That is all? You do not see anything for me, maybe, Bubbe? Where are we going? What is going to happen to us? I'm scared! Aren't you ever scared?" I threw myself into her arms and tried to think of my violin so I would not cry.

"Yes, my sweetest one." Bubbe stroked my head. "I see something, but I do not know if you want to hear."

I sat up and looked into her eyes. "Oh, yes, I do, please."

"It is an assignment I have for you."

"An assignment? What could it be?"

Bubbe held my chin in her hands and studied my face as though she were trying to make sure something was there, something one could not see, only feel, only know. "Remember, Chana," she finally said. "Remember everything. Remember, and have faith in God, always have faith."

I pushed away, slid off the bed, and stood before my window. "Bubbe, anyone could have told me that. I wanted you to use your gift. I wanted you to tell me what is going to happen to us."

"I've told you what you need to know, and it's all I know. The rest we all know, or can guess. Bad times are here, and worse are yet to come, but not tonight. Jakub is wrong about tonight, they will not come for us tonight."

"Remember everything," I said, more to myself than to her. "Remember, and have faith in God." I turned around but Bubbe was gone.

Again, I faced the window, and there on the other side was the girl I had seen just before Tata was shot. She had the same pain in her eyes and again she recognized me, knew me better than I seemed to know myself, and again I tried to understand. Who was she, staring in at me through the windowpane? Was she someone I should remember?

"Remember, and have faith in God," I whispered to her. "Always have faith."

CHAPTER SIX

Hilary

THE OLD LADY'S STANDING in front of me like she's waiting for me to say something. I don't. I just watch her and try
to remember. I can see the layers of skin beneath her eyes
sagging into her cheeks. Her arms dangle at her sides like a
couple of dead trout hooked to her sleeves. I know she should
be in bed.

Hey, where do you belong? Are you from the psycho ward?
You're sick. Stop watching me and go lie down.

Okay. Okay, don't. What do I care anyway?

Just so you know, it's not a dream. Yeah, I figured that
out.

It's all this fear, and not knowing, and dying. It's real,
it's . . . I won't be going back there, I can tell you. No one
controls me. Got that? I'm holding on, right here.

Hey, that's not my life. I'm not scared like that. I don't care
about those people. I don't care! They're nothing to me. So
stop looking like you know something, old bag lady. You don't
know anything.

Why is this happening?

Hah! I know what Mother would say. "It's God's way of
punishing you, baby. He's teaching you a lesson, and when
God's moving His hands through your life you had better sit
up and take notice."

Ever since Tata died — I mean, Daddy — since Daddy died, she's gone all religious. Everything is God's will, God's lesson, God's just punishment. Thing is, how come He's never punished her? How come she does something wrong and I get punished for it the rest of my life? How come all she has to do is get in good with the Lord and say "I'm sorry" and she's forgiven and I'm left still suffering?

It wasn't a dream. It was real with Mama and Bubbe and Zayde and them. Too real. It's like being out trick-or-treating and going into this haunted house and you tell yourself you're not scared 'cause it's Halloween. But then you find out it's not really Halloween at all and the house is for real. All those ghosts and all that evil — it's real. All that evil's for real.

You ever feel like your whole body's made of chalk? Chalk dust puffing inside your mouth? Your bones like teacher's brittle chalk sticks, and your heart just a hollowed-out chalky chamber?

Ever feel like that? Know what that's like, that emptiness? Well?

Until Brad, I felt like that every stinkin' day of my life. Ever since I was five.

My father was the only one who understood me. He was the one who taught me how to scramble eggs and how to spell my name and how to whistle through my thumbs and pick up sticks with my feet. He loved me and took care of me, not my mother.

Yeah, my mother spent the first five years of my life dragging around the house in her bathrobe. It always smelled like mustard and she had toilet paper crammed in all the pockets. She would take some of it out now and then and use it to dab at her eyes or blow her nose, especially after visiting with me. That's what they called it, my father and Grandmama — visiting.

"You must wash your hands extra well this morning, your mother will be down for her visit soon. You wouldn't want to put a grubby little hand in hers, would you?"

I don't think she ever noticed what my hands were like. Whenever I tried to take her hand she'd pretend she didn't see and stuff hers in her pockets with her soggy tissues.

Still, I always scrubbed them till they were pink and my nails were practically see-through, 'cause I always figured that someday she'd stop watching herself crying in the bathroom mirror and notice me, and when she did I wanted my hands to be ready.

"There is nothing but oppression within her.
As a well keeps its water fresh,
so she keeps fresh her wickedness;
violence and destruction are heard within her;
sickness and wounds are ever before me."

Do you hear her?

That's my freakin' mother. She's still here, still reading her Bible. I can't see her, but I can hear her.

Can you? Can you see her?

She's mad at me. Can you tell? She never comes right out and says it. She's never said, "Hilary, I'm mad at you for what you did." Instead she quotes the Bible, or better yet, just ignores me.

What the hell's she doing here, anyway? I don't need her. I've never needed her. Get rid of her!

Did you hear me? I don't want to hear her!

"Hear this, O foolish and senseless people,
who have eyes, but see not,

Who have ears, but hear not.
Do you not fear me? says the Lord;
Do you not tremble before me?"

If I keep talking, maybe I won't hear her. I'll just look at you and talk to you, all right?

Am I dying?

Why do I see only you?

Why is there nothing in this room?

Everything is white. The room is all lit up in bright whiteness and yet I can't see anything — except you.

I'm dying.

It wouldn't matter except for Brad.

You think he's here yet?

Oh, you don't think he's coming? Mother's full of it. He'll be here. Brad and me, we're the same, you know? Like after I hooked up with him all that chalk dust inside me just disappeared. Like it was just waiting for the right person to come along and blow it all away. Mother found religion and I found Brad. We're both looking for something to fill us up. What did she think, I'd choose her way? Can't get over it that her little Alice in Wonderland is hanging out with the Neo-Nazis. Like I've shamed her or something. I don't owe her. I don't owe her!

What's that? Hear that? That squeaking? It's moving around me.

"So how's the patient this morning?"

The nurse?

"The same, I guess. She doesn't move. Poor baby doesn't move."

I'm not a baby. I'm not your freakin' baby.

"You approve of this Neo-Nazi thing she's into?"

"No, but what can I do?"

"She must have picked it up somewhere. Must have learned it from someone."

"Well, not from me. I've never . . . We've never really understood one another."

"Ah! There's the problem."

"Yeah, always the mother's fault."

Silence.

"Actually, she probably joined up with her little gang of hate-mongers just to get my attention."

It's always you, isn't it, Mother? The world revolves around you. To get your attention? A stick of dynamite up your — your — nose wouldn't get your attention. You were always too into yourself to notice anything else. I was always knocking at your bedroom door to see if you needed any-thing — remember? Your spells? Right after Daddy died? Right after you gave me that speech about never leaving me again. Remember?

"Mommy, can I get you anything?"

"No. Go away."

"Are we going to eat dinner?"

"Later."

"But it's been dark a long time, I'm hungry."

"Later!"

"I'm hungry."

"Hilary, please, not now. Go away."

"Should I call the Reverend?"

"No, just get away from the door, okay?"

It always ended with me kicking her door and calling up the Reverend "Hi-call-me-Jonnie" Johnson. That's what I call him. It freaks my mother out. Hey, I learned how to dial his number before I learned how to spell my own last name. It was always Hi-Jonnie to the rescue.

"What could the good Lord have been thinking, leaving the two of us together?

"You know, when her father died she wore white to the funeral. She said it was what he wanted. I believed her. I believe he communicates to her from his grave — honestly.

"But then she kept on wearing white. She wore it until she was fifteen. Until she met that awful Brad boy. Every day. Every stitch of clothing had to be white, not cream, not ivory, but winter, ghostly, white. I know what you're thinking. I should have said something, done something about it. Thing is, I didn't feel I had the right."

That's because you *didn't* have the right. You left me! You left me! Can you believe it? Daddy dies and she has some kind of nervous breakdown and just walks out the door in the middle of the night and drives off with me screaming out my window after her.

"No, I didn't have the right. I never had the right to tell Hilary what to do. I never realized what a weak coward I was until she was born. And she's just like me. She doesn't know it, but she is."

I'm nothing like you! Nothing! I'm an Aryan Warrior, aren't I? I'm not going to listen to this crap.

"When she was born they put her in my arms and I looked down into that tiny face, that delicate pink face, and I knew I wouldn't be able to protect her. I knew that she'd get hurt someday and I would have no power to stop it.

"Truth is, she scared me. So tiny like that. Scared me so

much I couldn't go near her. Roy got his mother to come live with us. Just until I got over my fears. But the longer his mother stayed and the more she took over, the more frightened I became. I was no mother to Hilary. She didn't need me. None of them did. And when Roy died I begged her grandmama to stay on. I begged her to take care of Hilary, but she was too ill, too old."

Yeah, I remember that sweet scene. You and Grandmama start fighting after the funeral. Right after the stinkin' funeral. The taxi's waiting to take Grandmama away and you're fighting over the stupid luggage. You're tugging on the suitcase like you want to make a trade, you'll keep the luggage if she'll take me. But both of you want the luggage. Too bad you lost, huh, Mother?

Then like two nights later you run off to some hotel for three days. Three days! And I'm left alone in that house with just your crusty old jar of mustard, less than half a loaf of bread, and some old sour milk for food. And get this, Grandmaw, she leaves me a note on the refrigerator door. A note! If she knew anything about kids, anything at all, she'd know a five-year-old can't read some letter written in cursive.

I spent the whole time staring out my bedroom window, singing and talking to my stuffed dog, Whimper. Really. I still remember the songs. One was about Daddy's flowers bent over crying in the backyard, and another was about Grandmama's sweater with the hole hole hole left in my room room room, and at night I sang about Mr. Funny Sunny Sun.

I stayed up through the first night right there in that chair and watched the furniture and toys grow so big I thought they'd swallow me. The flowers on my wallpaper turned into these lips with fangs that dripped blood, and the toys and dolls on my shelves became live, breathing spiny creatures that whispered and laughed—You're all alone, there's no one left. No one.

By the third day I knew she wouldn't be coming back, but I couldn't leave my place at the window. I was waiting for Daddy. I just knew he'd come. He always came. Always when I needed him. I knew he'd come back before I finished all the bread. But then the hours of that third day passed and I was so hungry I just kept eating. I was down to a little square of bread and I was just picking at it, eating just a crumb at a time, giving Daddy time to get there. But then she comes back. She comes rushing into my bedroom and finds me staring out the window.

I was watching this little boy, this baby, laughing and clapping hands with his father. They were the new people who had moved in behind us. I couldn't look away. Mother kept grabbing me and shaking my arms, but all I wanted to do was watch that baby—baby Simon and his father with the funny little beanie cap on. I kept trying to twist away from her. I knew if I didn't keep watching they'd disappear, and while she was holding me, holding my face, they did, they disappeared. That happy laughing father just disappeared.

She didn't care. What the hell did she care? She wanted me to listen to her. She kept talking, with her eyes all shining like silver spoons and telling me all about some Gideon's Bible in a hotel room and something about suicide, like I knew what that meant. Telling me how the Lord made her see the light and how she was forgiven and how she was going to make it all up to me. How she was never going to leave me again.

Right. She could never make that up to me. Never. She can't get off so free and easy-breezy like that.

"Of course the children at school teased her at first, with her wearing all that white every day, but then they just forgot about her. She simply blended into the schoolroom like a forgotten piece of chalk. You can imagine my first parent-teacher conference, with me sitting in one of those tiny chairs pulled up to the teacher's desk while the teacher sits towering above me in her teacher's chair.

" 'Frankly, Mrs. Burke,' she says in this hoity-toity voice, 'I can only show you her work, I don't know your daughter in any other way. Dicky Reilly, now, he and Pete Dennis are troublemakers. Then there's the little girls' social group that has its ups and downs throughout the day that I've got to supervise, and of course, the class projects. Well, as you can guess, it's quite easy to overlook a quiet little miss who does what she's told and turns in a neat paper.'

"Really, that's the way she talked, all superior and making sure I understood it wasn't her fault she didn't know Hilary even existed. So who's fault was it? Mine? Then I ask her if Hilary has any friends, and she's real cagey, not really answering me, just saying, 'She doesn't seem to talk, now, does she?' Saying it as if she thought Hilary couldn't talk, like she didn't know how! Then she says how she felt Hilary needed to see the school psychologist. A psychologist! At six years old, mind you. Well, I told her. I said I didn't believe in any of that psychological mumbo-jumbo, and if my baby was in trouble she could just talk to the good Lord. God would show her the way. And you know what? I never went back."

"To that teacher?"

"No, Nurse — what is it — Fulbright? No, I never went back

to that teacher, that school, or any other school. I hate schools, always have."

See what I mean? My mother doesn't go to school to see how I'm doing because she's always hated school. It has nothing to do with me. I don't see a psychologist because she doesn't believe in them. I'm expected to talk to the "good Lord," but why? What good has it ever done? He's never talked back.

"Thus says the Lord:
 Stand by the roads, and look,
 and ask for the ancient paths,
 where the good way is; and walk in it,
 and find rest for your souls."

I don't want to hear it, Mother.

I hear the clinking of glass and a quick ripping sound. Something inside me shifts and shivers as though a cold shot of quicksilver has gone surging through my veins.

"Look at her. I always liked it best when she was asleep. I could look at her then. I could know her then, or at least pretend I could. She's so small and thin, and pale. Not because she's dy—hurt, but just naturally. Just like Alice in Wonderland, she is. People always said that. And until she met up with Brad, she always lived on that other side of the looking glass, in her own world, never bothering to look out at us—at me."

You got that right, Mother. I always felt like Alice on this crazy, mixed-up, upside-down, inside-out planet. And why should I have looked out from my world? Would you have been there if I had?

"When I'd come home from work at night I used to stop outside her bedroom door. It was always closed. I could hear her though, singing. She and her father were always singing together. He sang bass in the choir at church. When Hilary was born, I dropped out of the choir, but he kept going, and on those Sundays when he had a solo, even when she was an infant, he'd have someone bring her upstairs to hear him sing. She loved it. She loved the sound of his voice.

"Now I sing in the choir at a different church. She's never heard me. She has my voice, not his."

Daddy dies and suddenly you're in that wacko church all the time, drooling over every word Reverend "Hi-call-me-Jonnie" bellows. Then you start parading around with a Bible and quoting Scripture, and going on retreat and to choir rehearsals and anywhere but home to your empty house. Empty except for that white lump of nothing crumpled on the floor upstairs.

You took God away from me. I knew God when I was five. I could hear Him when I was five. But then you turned religion into a performance, a three-ringed circus with a new trinity — Father, Mother, and holy "Hi-call-me-Jonnie" — clowns, all of you.

"It's the church that saved me. It's God who's given me strength and courage. If Hilary makes it, I hope she can find God someday. She thinks she's so powerful, so indestructible, hanging out with those hoodlums. She doesn't know how weak she is. All that hiding behind her clothing, behind her 'Heil, Hitlers,' behind her fear. She's weak. Like I was. She's just like I was."

That's crap, Mother. Pure crap, and I refuse to listen to it.

"To whom shall I speak and give warning,
  that they may hear?
  Behold their ears are closed,
  they cannot listen;

behold, the word of the Lord is to
them an object of scorn,
they take no pleasure in it."

Grandmaw, are you here? I can't see you. Everything is fading. Everything is spinning. I don't want to go back there — please!

CHAPTER SEVEN

Chana

EVERYTHING WAS AT FIRST MISTY and unclear. I was walking through a thick, steamy grayness and all around me I could hear the footsteps of others, perhaps hundreds of others. Out of all of those footsteps, I began to pick up my mother's very even, rhythmic steps, and my grandmother's, quick, and heavy on the heels. I kept walking, not seeing, only hearing and smelling and feeling. The air, with its sharp odor of souring decay, stung my eyes and made tears stream down my face. I blinked and blinked, squeezing out the stinging and trying to focus on what I was pulling behind me. What was I holding? My hand was hot and sweaty. I felt skin against my skin and realized I was holding little Anya's hand in mine and pulling her along, following the sour odors like a dog.

My back was bent with the bundle I was shouldering, and my right hip felt bruised by what could only be the end of my violin case thumped against me as I walked. I wanted desperately to set the bundle down and plunk myself on the ground, but I could not. There were soldiers. I could hear their sturdy boots slamming down on the cobbled road behind me. I could hear their shouts of *"Schneller, schneller!"* as they tried to hurry us along, faster and faster. I picked up my pace and Anya groaned beside me. I looked down and I could see her. Through the clearing mist and my own tears, I could see her dark head bobbing up and down as she trotted along, trying to keep up.

"It cannot be much longer," I whispered to her. She squeezed my hand and looked up at me, her eyes wide, her lips pressed between her teeth. I tried to smile.

"Poor Zayde," she said after a little silence. "Will he die, do you think?"

I looked ahead of us to search out Zayde's small gray head in the crowd of weary people trudging along in straggled lines. I found him at last lying huddled against the wall of the cart we used to carry our belongings. Jakub was pulling the cart and carrying a bundle on his back as well. Beside him, on either side of the cart, were Mama and Bubbe, each with her own bundles and suitcases, whispering prayers for Zayde.

At seventy-one, he was twenty-one years older than Bubbe and looked even older. Like Tata, he had a weak heart that would beat frantically against his chest anytime he strained himself or whenever he was overtired. We were all surprised he'd lasted as long as he had, all of us except Bubbe, who said that his will to live was so strong he might bury us all first.

I hurried up alongside Mama and the cart. "Mama, he is lying so very still," I said as I looked down at the thin gray man who resembled my grandfather only slightly.

"It is all right, Chana. He will be all right. It is just rest he needs."

I was not sure I believed Mama, but I wanted to and I tried to sound cheerful when I said, "We will all be all right as soon as we can get to our new home and wash this mud off."

I frowned at my cold and soaking feet. It was early spring and all around us the snow was melting and had turned the ground to mud. As people dragged past us, their feet would splatter the mud onto our legs. At first there were apologies, but as we continued to walk on the uneven pavements, everyone with their loads on their backs and in their arms, the apologies became fewer and fewer, until people neither noticed nor cared. All around us people kept tripping, stubbing their toes into the cobblestones and broken pavement, and landing, with their bundles flying, in the clinging black mud. By the time we arrived at our destination — the poorest, dirtiest part of Lodz, called Baluty — we all looked as if we belonged there.

I swallowed hard as we squeezed along the narrow streets, past rows of ugly, crumbling, sagging houses. Which one would be ours? I wondered. I heard Anya whimper, and I saw her worried expression as she looked up at Mama.

Mama patted her head. "Just think, the people who used to live here all survived, and if the Germans had not chased them out, they'd be here still. They have had to live in poverty all their lives. They have no money and no education. They could not take care of their homes. But just wait and see how we fix up ours. If the Nazis want to stick all the Jews into one little corner of the world, well . . . we will show them what we can do with the garbage dump they have put us in."

At last we arrived at our apartment. Had it been assigned to us? I wondered. By whom? The new Chairman? I had heard about a man here named Chaim Rumkowski. As we scrambled and trudged through the mud and the streets, we would catch bits of conversation about this man — our new leader. He was called the Chairman of the Jews, but the Nazis were the ones who gave him the position. Would he work for us, or for them? Everyone wanted to know. Already there were rumors good and bad about this man, some people spitting as they said his name and others speaking of him as if he were a king — "So good to the little orphans," they would say. He frightened me. Anyone having to do with the Nazis did. He would take orders from the Nazis — how could that be good?

Zayde was struggling to climb out of the cart, while Jakub was struggling to keep him in it and carry the cart upstairs.

"Jakub, it is too much. I am not dead yet. Now let me walk."

Jakub's eyes teared up. "Please, Zayde, let us do this. You are making it more difficult and already you are overtired."

"So, *now* it is you decide to think of this family. *Now* you think of me. Let me out, I will walk."

"No!" Jakub burst out as he dumped the bundle from his back onto the floor. "I am thinking still of me, Zayde. If you die, I will be— I will be the man of the family." He paused and then whispered, "Please, Zayde, I need you."

Zayde humphed and turned his head away, falling against the wall of the cart. "Then find someone to help you," he finally said.

At long last we hoisted Zayde over some friendly stranger's shoulder and hauled him and all the belongings we had brought with us up to our new home. I wanted to throw my exhausted body down on a bed or a chair, but the sight of our home — our room — left me standing on my wobbly legs in the doorway.

"I am not going in," I said as my mother and grandmother dragged the load from the cart across the room. "Where are we all to sleep? There is nothing here! How will we live in this place? Even *you* cannot fix this, Mama. Look!"

She looked. We all did.

There was just the one room for all six of us. The walls were so smudged with dirt and soot it was hard to make out their true color. A table with the front legs shorter than the back stood in the center of the room with two green and two brown chairs pulled up to it. Looking beyond the dirt and litter that cluttered the rotting, sloping floor, I spotted two cots, both tipped over on their sides. The ceiling sloped down toward us but showed no evidence of imminent collapse.

Mama rushed to the windows and flung them open while Bubbe helped Zayde over to one of the cots that Jakub had righted. From my spot in the doorway I caught a glimpse of the view through the windows before Mama slammed them shut again. The back of our room overlooked one of the refuse heaps, which was overflowing and crawling with rats. I shuddered.

"Mama, we cannot live here," I said, thinking that somehow she and Bubbe would figure out a way to get us all back home. "Really, we cannot."

Mama was not listening. She opened the only door in the room besides the entrance and discovered a small, greasy kitchen.

"*Nu*, we are here," she said as she turned and faced us all, her body sagging against the little cookstove. "Jakub, I want you to find us some water. Anya, sweep the litter into a corner, and Chana, run and see if you can find where the Hurwitzes have settled; they cannot be far."

I was glad to get away, to get back outside and see life, such as it was, streaming before me. People were still coming, young and old, laden with unruly bundles bursting with pots and bowls, irons and brushes and blankets. *Droshkies*, horse-drawn wagons, clopped by, carrying sick, gray-faced people, with dogs yapping at the wheels as they wobbled over the cobblestones. I stepped out into the street as an elderly woman leaned over the edge of one of the wagons and vomited. It landed on the lower half of my dress and on my shoes. I cursed her and then, shocked by my own behavior, began to cry as I roamed the street, forgetting what or who I was even looking for. I stumbled along with the crowd, full of self-pity, ignoring the children smaller than I who bravely scrambled along beside their parents without complaint. I hated them. I hated everyone and everything, and if one more person so much as splattered one more clump of mud in my direction I swore I was going to . . .

"Chana!" I heard someone call. "Chana! Up here, child."

I looked up and saw Mrs. Liebman waving from her window as though she were watching a circus parade passing by, and perhaps she was.

"Hello!" I called up. "I — I am looking for the Hurwitzes. Have you seen them?"

"You will not find them with your face on the ground. A hug and a cool cloth are what you need. Then you find your Hurwitzes."

I suddenly longed to throw myself into Mrs. Liebman's arms and feel her plump body, like so much eiderdown, swallow me, comfort me, protect me. I rushed up the stairs and found her waiting for me in the doorway of her home.

"Chana." Mrs. Liebman held out her arms and I ran to them, sobbing. I let her rock me and soothe me, her voice washing over me like the gentle waves of a lake. "Shh, it is all right now. Shh, it is all right."

Eventually, I became aware of other voices coming from behind her. I opened my eyes and saw her daughter, little Gitta, staring up at me with her head tilted to one side, her left hand tugging at her mother's dress. I pushed away from Mrs. Liebman and rubbed away the remains of my tears with the sleeve of my dress.

"I am sorry," I said as I backed away from them. "You have your own family — sorry." I looked over Mrs. Liebman's head and saw the rest of her family, all nine of them, crowded into a room that looked even smaller than ours.

"We are all of us family now, Chana. You understand?"

"Yes."

"Let us clean you up then. With such a mess the Hurwitzes would not recognize you."

I allowed her to lead me into the room — their home — already scrubbed clean but so crowded with family and belongings there was little space for us to move around. As she rubbed me clean with a cloth dipped from time to time in a bucket of water, we exchanged stories.

I learned that the Germans had chased them from their home just over a week ago. They were almost the first from our neighborhood to arrive in the ghetto. I could not believe it when Mrs. Liebman said that already the ghetto had been cleaned up considerably since they had arrived. I marveled, too, at the high spirits of the whole Liebman family. The younger children were running up and down the stairs while older ones stood around and chatted. Many were laughing, and others were looking out the window to the street below.

Mr. Liebman caught my quizzical glance and smiled. "It is good now, Chana. No more killings and riots. No more chasing us off the streets and rounding us up to clean the walls and dig ditches. We can look after our own again. It is crowded, yes, but they leave us alone. It may not be such a bad thing, this building of a wall around our ghetto, if it keeps the Nazis out. The Chairman, he has already begun plans for rebuilding the workshops and factories, so it is good. Relax and smile, and have some sausage." Mr. Liebman stabbed a chunk of sausage onto his fork and held it out to me.

I could not remember the last time I had eaten. I thanked

him and grabbed the sausage, greedily stuffing it in my mouth and smiling as they laughed at my bulging cheeks.

Someone called up from the street below, offering a game of cards outside, and the whole family charged down the stairs. Mrs. Liebman and I and the baby, whom I now saw for the first time asleep on a rug in the corner of the room, were the only ones left. I thought about what Mrs. Liebman had said. We were all family now — all of us together, living on top of one another, crowded into one section of the city, all Jews, all hated, but all a family. I knew this was important. I needed to remember this. I needed to save my own anger and hate for the people on the other side of the fence. The woman who vomited so ungraciously on my dress was my family, and I vowed to be nicer to everyone I saw, everyone I came in contact with. And I vowed to remember this day, and this thought, and this moment alone with Mrs. Liebman, always.

CHAPTER EIGHT

Chana

MY WORLD SPUN FORWARD, flinging me headlong into the midst of ghetto life. I felt my life before the ghetto, with Tata, and our home, and being warm and well fed, had been but a fantasy. I could hardly remember anything outside of the ghetto. Surely I had lived here all my life, gone to school here always, scraped for food always — always starving, always dirty, always sick.

Anya, little Anya, had proved to be the strong one. She was cheerful, resourceful, and generous. Beside her, I felt mean and greedy.

It already seemed a long time ago, the late spring of 1940, when they sealed off the ghetto and I joined the *Hachschara*; a special training group. Back then, still the early days, I was determined to ignore the barbed wire that wrapped around our packed and dirty city like sausage casings, guarded by Nazis at every post, and become a part of this clean-up crew. A man named Jakub Poznanski divided us into small groups and showed us how to work the soil and plant grass and flowers. We even managed to find some benches to dot about our little parks. My hopes were high back then, and no one was prouder than I when on one sunny Sunday afternoon all of us in the various *Hachschara* groups paraded before the Chairman, some three thousand of us, chanting and singing and marching to the Hebrew commands.

Of course, back then we were not yet starving. Things changed quickly though, and soon we found ourselves without potatoes and other vegetables, without meat, with little more than some stale black bread, soup, coffee, and butter. For these we waited in long lines that straggled down the block and around the corner. We were tired, angry, and irritable. My resolve to treat everyone as my family faded, then disappeared with the food, as did the muscles in my arms and legs, and the belief that I would survive all of this, that everything was going to be all right.

Zayde and Jakub worked on Brzezinska Street in the new shoe factory. They worked with the finest leather, fashioning it into high-quality shoes for men and women and boots for the soldiers. The shoes were all taken and sold outside the ghetto. No one inside could buy them. We walked around in the same old shoes with the soles worn through.

Each day, Zayde returned from the factory looking a little shorter, a little thinner, and complaining of sore toenails and back pains. We laughed at first. Zayde and his toenails. If that is the worst of his problems, he will be all right, we told each other. We did not know then that it was a sign of the body deteriorating, of starvation. It wasn't until the Krengiels, a couple transported from Russia, moved in with us that we learned all the signs and symptoms of every disease imaginable.

Mr. Krengiel was a tall, heavy man in his forties who wore a beard, had a balding head, hypochondria, and a whine that drove me crazy in any language.

Mrs. Krengiel was neither short nor tall, fat nor thin. She would have been nondescript right down to her personality if it were not for her bright silver hair and the chocolate egg-shaped mole on her left cheek.

Mama had said that we had to be nice to them.

"They are, after all, foreigners who have been plunked down in a strange place, separated from family and friends. It is the least we can do."

We all tried our best to be nice. Jakub and Zayde found Mr. Krengiel a job at the factory, and Mama taught the couple English and German at night. We even offered to give up one of the two cots because Mama believed that each family should have one. They were not thankful.

"It is silly for such a young healthy family to take a cot when it is obvious we are both not well," said Mr. Krengiel.

"You are forgetting Zayde and Bubbe," Mama said, trying to keep her voice level. "Both are older than you."

"Perhaps, but Bubbe is so healthy, and as you can surely see, we are not." Mr. Krengiel sat down on one of the cots and gripped the edge as if to say, You will have to pry me out.

Mama looked tired. She had had enough. Her cheeks were sunken and her eyes so far away, setting back farther and farther in her head, with only brown circles marking where they used to be.

"You may have one cot." She sighed. "But Zayde will have the other. Even you must see that he can barely hold himself up."

"Zayde, pardon my honesty, but Zayde will be dead soon anyway. What does it matter now where he sleeps? There is no comfort for him now except in heaven."

Mama held down her anger. The man was crazy, irrational. We were all just grateful that Zayde, Jakub, and Bubbe were not there to hear this. We knew that this crazy man would have said the same thing in their presence.

"Each family will have one cot, Mr. Krengiel," Mama said through clenched teeth. "You are free to do with yours as you please. However, Zayde will be occupying the other and there is no room for discussion." She turned her back to him and held her head high, her shoulders tense, waiting for the next insane remark. But he was silent.

Instead, every morning and every night, Mr. Krengiel groaned, complaining of the cold, the stiff back he got from lying on the cot and working at the factory, and his swollen feet — "a sure sign of starvation." If he wasn't whining about his body, he was dragging out some old letter from his cousin who had fled to America two years earlier. He would read aloud the same tired passages, and then look up at us with wonder in his eyes as if he were reading them for the first time.

"In America, the sandwiches you can get you cannot imagine," he would then say to us. "Fresh *white* bread thick with sardines, sauerkraut, and three kinds of cheeses, and can you guess how much something like that costs? Can you, Chana?" He'd poke me in the stomach. "Can you, Anya?" Another poke. "A nickel! Oy! A nickel! You know what that is? You know what a nickel is?" Poke, poke.

We could not understand the man. He arrived fat and got no thinner as the days passed, no matter that he ate no more than the rest of us. But one night I watched as he lay on the cot with his wife sleeping on the floor below him. I knew he was awake because his nose was not whistling. The moon shone into the room, a giant beam highlighting his corner of the room, making it glow, making him glow as he rose from the bed, carefully stepping over his wife. He looked like a ghost all silver and white moving in and out of the shadows as he crossed the room. I closed my eyes as he made his way toward me, pausing at times to listen — for what? I waited until I heard him pass and opened my eyes again. He was heading toward the kitchen! I knew instantly what he was going to do. It all made sense now. Every morning we would all say how our imagination would play tricks on us at night and that the remains of our loaves of bread would grow bigger in our minds as we slept, only to grow smaller when we woke. It had not been our imagination at all. It was fat Mr. Krengiel stealing bits of bread from each of our loaves!

I waited until I was sure he was into the bread before jumping up. "Mr. Krengiel!" I shouted. "How dare you! You *chozzer!* Stealing our food while we starve to death."

By this time everyone was awake, and Jakub was about to strike the greedy man when Bubbe came up from behind and gently touched Jakub's arm.

"No, Jakub. Let him explain," she said.

"What can there be to explain? Stealing our bread — Zayde's bread." Jakub nudged Mr. Krengiel. "Look at my grandfather. Look at him! How dare you take his food!"

Mr. Krengiel looked and then sank to the floor as though his bones had turned to liquid.

Jakub turned a helpless face to Bubbe. "What is he doing now?"

Bubbe rushed forward, calling out commands over her shoulder. "Get some water, any water, and someone help me get him to the cot."

Jakub swore under his breath and helped Bubbe lift the limp body up off the floor. "He is pretending. You know he is pretending."

Bubbe turned a cold eye toward Jakub and said through gritted teeth, straining beneath the weight of the man, "Do not say things you may regret, child. It is hard enough living here without adding guilt to your load."

They dropped him on his cot and only then did we notice that Mrs. Krengiel was still asleep.

All of us had gathered around the two of them, Mama with the dish of water, Zayde sitting upright on his cot, Anya and I next to Bubbe and Jakub. Who could speak? We all knew Mrs. Krengiel could not have slept through all the noise we had been making. She was faking, we knew, but we said nothing, waiting for Bubbe to make the first move — and she did.

Crouching down on the floor, she tapped Mrs. Krengiel's shoulder and whispered, "You must get up now, dear, your husband needs you. He is very ill."

Slowly she rolled over and, looking dazed, opened her eyes and sat up. "What is it? What are you all doing? Surely it cannot be morning yet."

In the morning Bubbe took Mr. Krengiel to the hospital where she was working as a nurse. We all felt it was nonsense. Letting Mrs. Krengiel pretend she was asleep so she would not get blamed for her husband's greed was one thing, but going through all the trouble to haul Mr. Krengiel across town to the hospital was another. What good could it do? The farce had been carried too far and we all said so, but Bubbe stood firm and off he went.

Mr. Krengiel was there for four weeks and during that time we all went back to our usual existence of starving, working, and studying. Even little Anya had found herself a job.

Both of us were supposed to attend school. At first, we walked along together to the building where classes were held, but eventually we found our own friends, some old, some new, and we separated at the first corner and walked to school with them. I never thought about not seeing Anya around anymore. There were more and more students every day as new arrivals from Holland, Russia, Germany, and even France entered the ghetto.

Then Anya began to bring home an extra ration of bread or a potato and sometimes extra money, claiming that people would give it to her on the streets.

"This is nonsense," Mama said. "No one simply hands out food and money. Anya, you must be truthful."

"But, Mama, I hand out food and money to the sick people lying in the streets."

"You are not sick. You are not lying in the streets. Anya, if you are sneaking beneath the wires, I will drop dead now with the heart attack. They will beat you or even shoot you if they catch you outside the walls."

"No, Mama. It is as I said, people give it to me, and I give some to the others and bring the rest home for Zayde." Anya lowered her eyes. "He is so ill, Mama. The wind someday will blow him away."

Mama gave up asking her, but none of us believed her story.

One night, Mama asked me to follow her to school the next morning to see that she did not go under the wire.

The two of us set off together that next day with the sun rising high in the icy sky. The roads were slick with yesterday's rain. We walked carefully through the mud, tucking our bread under one arm, our books under the other, and jamming our hands into our pockets. At the end of the block we separated as usual, but as Anya made her way down a narrow side street, I turned back around and followed her. She scurried along the streets, her body swaying, her hair swinging side to side, the way it did whenever she felt especially important or grown-up. She seemed so small, retreating down yet another street and turning right, small and fragile and innocent. I wanted to rush up and cover her with my arms, wrap my coat around her delicate body, and keep her warm, but I knew she would have none of it. Despite her appearance she was feisty and strong, and more apt to be putting her arms around me, and wrapping her coat around some poor *shlepper* passed out in the mud, than accepting help for herself.

She stooped before a broken window located at the base of a crumbling building and pulled out something stashed inside. It was a large iron hook, rusty and heavy, judging by the way she was carrying it. She left her books inside the window and hurried away. I followed her out toward the cemetery and, worse yet, toward the large, foul-smelling garbage fields crowded with people dressed, partially dressed, and completely naked, down on their knees digging. As she climbed one of these heaps of refuse, ignoring the rats and discarding her coat and dress in a pile with the others, she was greeted by those of her friends who had arrived there before her. After hugs of hello they returned to work, Anya beside them with her iron hook, as intent and solemn as a little old man panning for gold.

I couldn't believe what I was seeing. Here was a whole other world that I had never seen, or perhaps had chosen not to see. Observing them now, I saw them perhaps as an outsider might see them, as the Germans would see them — filthy Jews, digging around in their own garbage, their own excrement.

One woman gleefully held up the tiniest bit of coal, another an old rag, and still another a sliver of wood, all gold to them, almost priceless. It was, for most of them, their lifeline.

Men trudged by with thick bands of rope wrapped around their waists or over and around their shoulders, their bare feet pushing against the ground, leaning forward, heaving and pulling giant wagons of excrement. They were the fecal workers, the ghetto's beasts of burden. They came through our gutterless streets once or twice a week, cleaning up, helping us to keep typhus and other deadly diseases at bay. Perhaps, I thought to myself, standing there in front of the "fields," I owe my life to them, my health—and yet I had ignored them. They were, in my mind, the excrement they cleaned up. They were the people we pretended did not exist, the same way we pretended not to see our neighbors and friends squatting down in the streets to relieve themselves, the same way we pretended not to be doing it ourselves.

As I looked at them now, sweating on this cold, windy day, their overalls flapping against their emaciated bodies, I whispered, "You, I will remember. You are important to me."

Mama was not happy to hear about Anya skipping school to go digging up coal and selling it to people only slightly better off than we were. She had planned to have it out with her when Anya returned home, but Zayde got there first. He was home early from the shoe factory, claiming it was too painful to sit.

"My bones, they must be dissolving," he said, and then tried to laugh it off. "Chana, it is magic. I sit down one day and my bones are there, another day, *pfft!* They are gone."

I helped Mama lower him onto the cot. He was shivering. I ran and grabbed up all the blankets we had and began placing them one by one on top of him.

"No! It is too painful. It hurts, Chana. Please, no blankets."

I looked at Mama. What were we to do? He was freezing and yet the blankets were too heavy for him.

"Lie down next to him," Mama said.

I stared down at Zayde, quivering on the cot, his skin shiny, waxy, almost colorless. I decided I had heard Mama wrong and looked up at her, waiting.

Mama nodded. "Go on, child, lie down. Your body heat might help."

I did as I was told while Mama made a tent over us. She placed a chair at each corner of the cot and spread the blankets out over and across us. Then she tucked them under the legs of the chairs.

It was a cozy little tent, dark and private, something Anya and I would have enjoyed together, but Zayde and I? I closed my eyes and listened to Zayde's shallow breathing.

He was whispering, *"Shema Yisrael, Adonai Elohainu Adonai Ehad."*

I whispered it, too, and realized that by its end he was no longer shivering. I turned my head and, with my eyes now accustomed to the dark, saw Zayde smile and then let out his breath. I turned away and stared up at the pattern on the blanket above us.

I laughed to myself as I saw the pattern move before my eyes. Mama was behind us in the kitchen, chopping up the frozen beets we had been given. The patterns shifted again and I could make out the shape of a face. It is like finding shapes in the clouds, I thought. Perhaps I am seeing the *Moshiah*. Perhaps he has come at last to save us, to tell us all will be well, bringing food — potatoes, and onions, and sausage, and butter. . . . The face lost its shadows and I saw it was not the *Moshiah* at all but my friend. I called her that now, the girl who saw me and knew me, and understood. She smiled down at me, a smile like Zayde's, and I tried to smile back but could not. I was cold, suddenly very cold, and I wondered if Zayde were cold, too. I reached out to touch his arm. Yes, he was cold, like an iron rod, cold and still, so very still. My zayde was gone.

Baruch dayan emet.

CHAPTER NINE

Hilary

I'M TRYING TO WIGGLE MY TOES, make something move. I need to get away, get out.

Nothing happens.

The old lady's standing with her face turned away so I'm staring at the back of her head. She's hardly got any hair back there, and what little's there is all pressed and matted. I can see a scar, too, like a strip of seersucker running down her scalp toward her neck. I don't want to look at it.

Bubbe?

Grandma? Turn around. What's wrong? Do you know something?

I'm so hungry. I feel as if something is chewing up my insides.

My zayde. I've lost my zayde. It feels like hunger. I can't tell them apart, sorrow and hunger — and pain. I think I'm hurting somewhere, everywhere, but I'm not sure. I just feel hungry — very, very hungry.

I need my mother. If you won't turn around, Bubbe, and speak to me, then please, go get Mama.

"Therefore I am full of the wrath of the Lord;
    I am weary of holding it in.
    Pour it out upon the children in the street,

and upon gatherings of young men, also;
both husband and wife shall be taken,
the old folk and the very aged."

No! I don't want to hear that! I don't want to hear her. She frightens me.

Why are you quoting those verses at me? You don't know. Why do you read as if you knew, as if you understood?

My zayde . . .

Why must people die? Why must the wrong people die?

Why didn't we die, Mother? Why did it have to be Daddy? And where is that greedy Jew boss who killed Daddy now? Is he living in some fancy mansion, bought with his blood money?

And the Germans — who guard the gates of the ghetto, who keep the food out and death in — will they ever suffer? Is there no punishment for them?

"They know no bounds in deeds of wickedness;
they judge not with justice
the cause of the fatherless, to make it prosper."

I don't understand. Can you hear me, Mother? Grandma, turn around. Someone explain what's going on. Why is she reading that passage to me?

I don't want to hear her. She's reading as though she and I were connected somehow, as if she knew about the Germans, about this other world.

Ah! Now you turn around.

You and I are connected, too, aren't we, Grandma? Only

I don't know how, or why. And why should Mother and I be connected? She never wanted me and I never needed her, so why—why must we be connected?

Am I wicked?

Is it wicked to hate people who have destroyed your life? Is it wicked to hate people whose sole purpose is to make your life miserable?

Does Simon hate me? How long have I been here? How long can a person live without food? Why did I have to know him? Why did he have to move in behind us right before Daddy died? What kind of sick joke is that? Moving a Jew family, a happy, smiley Jew family into my life? I don't want to be connected to him. I don't want to care about him. I don't care.

I hate it. I hate it all!

I hate the Jews! And the Germans! And while I'm at it, I hate you, Mother! And I hate being trapped in this white place with you, Grandma, Grandmaw, with your droopy-dog look.

I hate living in the ghetto, and starving to death, and watching the people I love die.

I hate it all! All I feel is hate—all I am is hate.

Just let me close my eyes. No more thinking. No seeing.

Just let there be darkness.

And silence.

Just let me not be.

Who's that? I hear someone. Is it Brad? Brad's here. I told you he'd come.

"How is the patient?"

"Reverend Jonnie! I'm so glad. I didn't think they'd let anyone else up here, but of course, you're her pastor."

Never, Mother! Never a pastor who glides through life on his own oil slick.

"What's the news on the outside? Have they found that boy?"

"I'm sorry, Ruby. No, the news isn't good. The parents received a note in their mailbox last night. It said the boy is dead. No signature, of course, just a swastika."

"Good Lord, the poor kid. And Hilary . . ."

It's not true. It's not. Grandma, don't believe him. They wouldn't do that. Brad wouldn't do that. It's not true. Oh, please, it's not true.

Stupid Simon. Why'd he have to be so stupid? Why'd he have to be so little, so different?

I asked him that once. No really, I did. We were in the garden between our houses. He was working, weeding around the vegetables and grinning like he was having fun. That's when I asked him why he was so weird, why he had to act so different so nobody liked him. Know what he said to me? He said, "I thought you liked me." That's how stupid he was—is.

I told him I didn't like him, and neither did anyone else. And he says, "You used to like me. You used to play with me, remember?"

"That was because I was bored," I told him. "I could never like a Jew boy. You're all snobs."

"We're not snobs, you just don't understand us. Why don't you try to understand us? Why don't you read your Bible, then you'll understand."

"See," I said, "that's just what I mean, Jew boy."

I kicked a clump of dirt at him. I mean, who acts like that? Who talks like that? Only Simon. Simple Simon.

Oh, he's alive all right.

"Let's not worry about Hilary's future just now. How is she? What does the doctor say?"

"She just seems to be in this — limbo. I don't know if she's going to die or what. I don't think even the doctor knows."

"We must have faith, Ruby."

"Yeah, well, I brought my Bible."

"But you're upset. Come, sit back down and let's talk."

"It's just that it's not working. My prayers aren't working. There's no comfort in the words I'm reading, but I can't stop reading them. It's like someone else is choosing the words I have to read."

I thought you brought the Bible for me, Mama — Mother.

"Ah, God is speaking to you. You have been touched, blessed. We must get down on our knees and give thanks to God, who is preparing the way for what is to come."

"What are you saying? Is God preparing me for Hilary's death, or is He punishing me for it?"

"What do you think?"

"I've never been so frightened."

"Let us listen for God's precious words and He will give you the comfort you are seeking."

"No. Please, I don't understand. Why do I feel so compelled to read this book of Jeremiah? It's the Old Testament. I've never had any use for it, but reading it now, it frightens me. I feel as if the Lord is trying to tell me something.

"Tell me this, Reverend. Why should this passage frighten me so?

"And they have built the high place of Topheth, which is
in the valley of the son of Hinnom, to burn their sons and

their daughters in the fire; which I did not command, nor did it come into my mind. Therefore, behold, the days are coming, says the Lord, when it will no more be called Topheth, or the valley of the son of Hinnom, but the valley of Slaughter."

It frightens me, too.

Grandma? She's reading about the past, and yet it is also the future, isn't it?

"Perhaps you already know why this passage has special meaning for you. Do you? Ruby?"

"I'm not sure. It's as if these things are yet to happen. That's how I feel. A punishment, maybe, because of something I've done, or — or thought.

"I'm scared, Reverend."

You should be frightened, Mother. Not for your sake, but for mine. The words are a part of my present, my future. They're a part of that other world I keep spinning into. They're part of *my* punishment.

"And for what thought or deed do you fear God's punishment? He has long ago forgiven you for abandoning her. Let go of it, Ruby."

"But how can His forgiveness matter if Hilary won't forgive me? She's never forgiven me. There's so much guilt — I feel so much guilt for Hilary's life, a wasted life."

"It's *her* wasted life. She's chosen to waste it. She's chosen to hold on to her past and carry it with her like some banner of hate for the rest of her life."

"But it's my fault. I ruined her life."

"Let go of it, Ruby."

"I don't think I can. Sometimes — sometimes I think it would just be better if she died.

"Your ways and your doings
have brought this upon you.
This is your doom, and it is bitter;
it has reached your very heart."

I'm spinning back. Deep within my own head I'm spinning and the words from the Bible follow me. They follow me back into the darkness.

CHAPTER TEN

Chana

Your ways and your doings
have brought this upon you.
This is your doom, and it is bitter;
it has reached your very heart.

Words. I kept hearing words. They were Yiddish, and Polish and German, Russian and French; so many people crammed
into the ghetto and all of them speaking. They were talking
about death and fear and hunger and Hitler and God, but most
of all, they were talking about rules.

Rules! My head echoed with rules, ached with rules. There
were rules for everything, and every day that I survived, a new
rule was tacked onto the ever-growing list: No Jew can leave
the ghetto; children should not sell candy on the streets; Jews
should not eat in the soup kitchens but in their own homes; no
marriages, divorces, or funeral rites are to be performed; workshops are to remain open on Shabbos and Yom Kippur; one
thousand people are to report to 7 Szklana Street for resettle-
ment outside the ghetto at nine o'clock in the morning. . . .

We would all have gone mad if it were not for the jokes,
the ones that reminded us that we were all in this together.
Only *we* could understand the humor in the statement "You

cannot die, either, these days." There was no time to die, no place, and the rules almost forbade it and at the same time hurried it along. The daily death count rose steadily — twenty-five — thirty-five — sixty-five people dead: starved, diseased, killed, or suicided.

Zayde's death was one of many that February in 1942, and it was five days after his death before he was buried. His body lay discarded on the frozen ground with the others until a grave could be dug for him. We could not wash him or perform any of the traditional rites other than having Jakub recite the Kaddish, the prayer for the soul of the dead, as they lowered Zayde's body on two slats of wood into the ground.

It was a terrible time for Bubbe. There was no time for sitting *shiva*, no time for mourning. Each day was like the next, as though Zayde had just gone out for a loaf of bread and would be back soon. Bubbe went every day to the overcrowded hospital and returned home each night with news for Mrs. Krengiel about her husband. He was not a popular man there, but she did not tell his wife this. She only said that his condition remained the same. To us she said that he whined and begged and refused to budge from the bed.

"Today we all had enough of him," she told us one night after an impossibly long day on her feet. "All day long, calling out for food. 'Oy, Bubbe, some bread,' he says as I pass his bed. The others, they are ready to throw him out into the yard, from a window most likely, and I do not blame them. We none of us have enough to eat, where does he think he is?"

We had never heard our Bubbe speak so harshly of anyone before, and I derived a guilty sort of pleasure from watching her lose her temper and become just as irritable as the rest of us. It was somehow good for me to see that even she was affected by the lack of food and the crowding and the constant work. Just staying alive had become a chore, and some days, almost more work than we could handle.

I could no longer concentrate on my studies; it had been days since I had been to school. All I could think about was food. Any other thoughts just made me cross. I would get my bread at the beginning of the week and by Wednesday I would have eaten it all. I would then panic, realizing that I might not eat again until the next week, but Anya always came through for me with some bit of something to eat each day. I was still too proud to go work with her in the "fields," but not too proud to take the food she got for it.

Sometimes, if I was lucky, I could sneak off to Krawiecka Street, to the House of Culture — a long, low building with a green roof that stood out among the grays and blacks of the other buildings. There I could almost forget I was starving.

The entrance was on the side of the building. If I got there early enough, I could enter without being seen and walk through the lobby and along a corridor to a small room where there was a hole in the ceiling. The hole was near the entrance to the room, and I could shinny up the door until my feet were resting on the doorknob and, with the door swung out just so, eventually push myself up and through the hole. Once there, I waited, sometimes hours, but it was always worth it. From my perch in the ceiling I could hear the violins, the cellos, the basses, and the violas playing Beethoven's Fifth Symphony. I could pretend I, too, was there rehearsing and performing for Mr. Theodore Ryder, the conductor. I could dream about the days before the war, before the ghetto, when Tata had arranged for me to audition for a local orchestra. It was not world famous, but I was by far the youngest member to ever audition for them, and wonder of wonders I got in! Tata was so proud. We had a celebration with all my family and friends. Mama made me a new dress to wear on performance nights. It was deep red, the color of beet juice. It was too big for me and I couldn't understand how it could be so big when Mama had so recently taken my measurements.

"Mama, it is so beautiful," I said as I twirled around for everyone to see. "But it is too big. You'll have to take it in."

"Chana, come here, child."

I eyed Mama from across the room. She shifted in her seat and glanced sideways at Tata. Tata merely hung his head.

"What is it, Mama?" I asked as I pirouetted over to her, the skirt flying out like a tutu. I curtsied before her and smiled. "Mama?"

"This dress is for next year, when you will be going into the orchestra. For when you are thirteen. That's not so long from now and you will be older then, more prepared. . . ."

"Thirteen! What difference will a year make? They accepted me now, for this year." I turned to face Tata. "Did they not, Tata? I am to go in this year, am I not?"

Mama got her way, not realizing there would never be a next year — not like we had planned. Tata was dead, and Zayde, and I was here in a hole in the ceiling. My violin, my treasure, was here in the ghetto, but I had not played it. I had picked it up after the *shiva* and had tuned it, but I could not play, nor could I cry for Tata. Another day, I told myself, but so far another day had not come.

The night after Bubbe had said those wonderfully wicked things about Mr. Krengiel, she came home so upset she could not speak. No one could get a word out of her, and she sat in the corner of the room with a blanket wrapped around her until Mrs. Krengiel returned home from her job in the straw factory.

Mrs. Krengiel took the news of her husband's death much

better than Bubbe, who after imparting the news sat back down and did not talk or eat the rest of the evening. She went on like this for days, returning each night from the hospital to sit in a corner with a blanket wrapped around her. She was praying, I think. I could sometimes hear a word or two, but she would speak to none of us, nor would she eat her dinner.

Mama was so upset by the change in Bubbe that she could not sleep at night. Instead she would watch Bubbe, who was still in her corner, refusing to sleep on Zayde's cot, insisting that Anya and I share it.

One especially cold night, we were all awake, listening to the distant sounds of the trains screeching and grumbling, the echo of boots slapping the pavement, of car horns and sirens, and drunken voices raised in song. It was strange to think this nightlife existed side by side with ours in the ghetto, a few mere strands of wire separating us, and yet it was enough. Those strands of wire sliced through our existence, dividing us up, life on one side, death on the other, heaven and hell shoulder to shoulder, never touching, never blending.

Anya kept turning over in the cot this way and that, and I was just about ready to kick her onto the floor when she got up on her own and went over to Bubbe's corner.

Bubbe was still sitting on the floor, knees to her chest, her head back against the wall. The moon spread its light across her blanketed feet, the quilted shapes, torn and dirty in the daylight, looking white and clean. Anya tried to whisper, but she had never been good at it, always thinking she was quieter than she really was, innocently giving away birthday and Chanukah surprises. I heard her whispering to Bubbe.

"Are you trying to die, too, Bubbe?"

Bubbe took her hand and rubbed it against her cheek. She whispered something to Anya and Anya wrapped her arms around Bubbe's neck and said, "Zayde's here with us, just like Tata and God and even Mr. Krengiel. You told me so, remember? And I did not believe you, but now I see them all at night when I close my eyes. I remember them, and Mosze and Nadzia, and I hear them talking to me. Do you, Bubbe? Do you hear their voices sometimes? I do. Even when I am digging I can hear them. When I am so hungry."

Bubbe held Anya in her lap and whispered to her. She spoke a long time, maybe all night, I do not know — I drifted off to sleep.

By morning Bubbe was her usual self, running late for the hospital and tossing kisses behind her as she and Jakub hurried off together.

Anya and I were already late for school, but it no longer mattered to us. Neither of us went to school anymore. It was easier to keep our minds off of food when we were physically active instead of sitting still in a classroom, listening to our stomachs rumble and watching our feet swell. Mama tried to convince us to keep up our studies, but she no longer had much control over us. Our lives had been turned upside down and she was forced to accept our choices, realizing that just having us home each night for dinner, still alive, was enough.

She could not even get that much from Jakub, who stayed out most nights. Sometimes he would come home in the early morning and stay only long enough to toss out bits of information before rushing off to the shoe factory. We all had our suspicions as to what he was doing, but we never dared voice them for fear that the Nazis might somehow overhear. As in the days after Tata's death, Jakub always had some new piece of information to impart, something no one else seemed to know. How did he know the movements of the war, where the Russians were, what decisions the English had made? He had to have access to a radio, and yet radios were illegal here in the ghetto. Newspapers were as well, but they were smuggled, often by small children, through the fence, and slipped along from one coat to another, read, and later used as wastepaper.

Bubbe had often seen Jakub coming out of the barbershop on her way to work, with his hair no shorter than the day before, and it was our growing belief that hidden somewhere in that shop was a radio. This we knew was dangerous enough, but Jakub, if it was true, did not stop at that.

One week he had been gone almost every night, not even returning in the morning before going off to work. Mama was convinced he was dead in spite of Bubbe's reports of seeing him, and she was just about to go looking for his body when he showed up with two boys in tow. The boys' names were Chajmek and Schmulek. They were brothers, the older one eighteen and the younger sixteen. It was evening and Jakub said he had to hurry away, but he wanted to leave the boys behind.

"What is this about, Jakub?" Mama asked, watching the two boys pacing the floor, each with a bundle on his back.

"They will only be here for an hour at the most," he said. "Do not worry, I will be back," and with that he was gone.

Schmulek, the older brother, stopped pacing and offered to help Mama with the soup as though there were vegetables to chop or barley to add. Mama refused but offered them each some of our food. I could feel my greedy old stomach begin to churn. They, in turn, refused, saying that they had plenty to eat in their bundles, and then resumed pacing, the younger one constantly wiping his runny nose on the sleeve of his coat. Something about this action repulsed me. Why, I was not sure. I had certainly seen far worse here in the ghetto, but it was enough to keep me from drinking my soup. I could not keep my eyes off them, and I was embarrassed when one or the other of them would look up and smile at me. I knew I was blushing, and I would try to look away, but a minute later I was watching them again, sure that they had once been quite handsome, before hunger had gnawed at their bodies and siphoned the color from their faces.

Anya must have been watching them, too, because she suddenly spoke up in a voice filled with surprise and delight. "Oy! They have no stars on their jackets!"

Chajmek and Schmulek dropped to the floor as though they had been shot. Anya put her hands over her mouth, Bubbe and Mama jumped up, and Mrs. Krengiel and I remained seated, staring.

Chajmek was the first to regain his composure. He gave us all an ingratiating smile.

"It is all right," he said. "Your son, he has gone to get us some. That is why we are here, hiding. We will bring you no trouble, we will be gone soon." He slid his eyes sideways for a glance at his brother.

We all looked at Bubbe. She would know if this was so.

Bubbe stepped toward the boys. "I think that you should not pace before the windows. And your bundles, they could be carried in such a way. . . ." She crouched down to adjust their things. "There, no one would know you have no stars." She turned away from them still smiling, but I could see sadness and worry in her eyes. She had touched them. She knew things about people after she had touched them. It was part of her "gift from God," as she called it, to know, and to see. She once tried to explain it to me, this "gift," as we were pasting photos into our photo album together.

"It is like this, Chana," she said. "I just empty myself of all thoughts, all concerns for myself, and then I reach out to the person before me. I touch him and look into his eyes and he shows me his past, who he is, and from that I can see his future. Yet sometimes, sometimes I feel it is a burden and not a gift at all."

"But why, Bubbe? To see so much, I think I would like it."

"Yes, it is good because in seeing them I understand them, and in understanding them I can love them, and in loving them I am closer to God. In that way it is a gift."

"Then how is it not a gift?"

"It is difficult to know so much about a person and yet be able to do nothing for him."

"But sometimes," I argued, "sometimes you can help?"

"I have learned, Chana, that it is usually best to let things alone, to let things take their natural course. Yes" — she nodded, more to herself than to me — "it is best that way."

Now Bubbe was walking back toward the table, her finger on her mouth, pensive, as though trying to make up her mind about something. Then she spun back around to face the boys. "Listen, stay here tonight. Do not leave. It is better that you stay, really it is. I shall speak to Jakub about it, he will understand."

"What will I understand?" Jakub asked, stepping into the room, his eyes bright, his hand tucked inside his coat.

Bubbe took Jakub's free hand in hers and looked into his face. "Not tonight, Jakub. It cannot be tonight."

He brushed her away, closing his eyes and turning toward the boys. "I know what I am doing, Bubbe. I have done it before."

Bubbe caught hold of his hand once more. "Yes, but not tonight, not with them."

Jakub spun around and glared at Bubbe. He said nothing.

Their eyes locked. The rest of us remained still, no one dared speak. I was not sure what this battle was about, but I felt certain Bubbe would win. Jakub knew better than to ignore her warnings.

"Jakub, I ask you one thing," she finally said. "Can you live with yourself if this fails?"

Jakub's nostrils flared. "It will not fail. I am not a child anymore. If you only knew the things . . . Never mind." He turned away, reached back into his jacket, and pulled out two flat paper parcels. He handed them to Schmulek and Chajmek. He then hugged the two brothers and said, "Hainik is waiting. Do not fret, it is good."

The boys thanked him, their uneasy expressions falling away. They turned to Mama and Mrs. Krengiel and thanked them as well, ignoring Bubbe, and then left. Jakub watched them go down the stairs and then came back into the room.

"You always said to have faith, Bubbe," he said, not looking at her but going to the table, serving himself some cold soup, and sitting down. "Where is your faith now? To many I am already a hero. They have faith. I have faith. And you, Bubbe, do you no longer have faith? Did your faith die with Zayde and Mr. Krengiel?"

Bubbe came over and stood behind Jakub's chair. She leaned over and with his face cradled in her hands kissed the top of his head. "Is it faith we are talking about, or ego? Perhaps you have faith in God. I know you have faith in yourself. But what about those boys? Could you put your faith in them? Did you think beyond the chance to once again be thought of as a hero? When Hainik leaves them at the wall, they will be on their own. Will they make it? Are they clever like you, Jakub?"

Jakub dropped his spoon into his bowl.

Bubbe continued talking. "I have learned that it is not

enough to have faith; we must know also where, and in whom, to put that faith. Where is your faith, Jakub? Is it with them tonight?"

The next morning, as I was walking toward the intersection of Smugowa and Franciszkanska streets, I saw the backs of two boys hanging on the other side of the barbed wire; both had been shot through the head.

CHAPTER ELEVEN

Hilary

I DON'T KNOW WHERE I AM. Everything is gray, as if I'm standing in a fog, the fog cast by the old woman in front of me. I stare at her and wonder. Is this Bubbe? Is it Grandma? Does it matter? I stare at nothing, into nothing, and wonder why I fight so hard to pull myself back through the hazy film that separates my two worlds. What's waiting for me?

Bubbe?

Grandma? I don't understand. Help me.

I don't know . . . my mind . . . I no longer know what's real. Is this my real life, here in this gloom, with you?

I see you. You smile at me. You cry. I can see your tears. Almost like — like you love me, but why? Why should you?

Why is it that I can only hold my mind here and know where here is when I'm staring at you, watching you? It's through you that I hear the others. It's through you that I'm living this — this life. Isn't it?

But why?

> "For thus says the Lord:
> Your hurt is incurable,
> and your wound is grievous.
> There is none to uphold your cause,

no medicine for your wound,
no healing for you."

I'm not ready to go, to — to die.

Mama? Mother?

You can't hurt me. You can't reach me.

I choose whether I live or die. Here I have a choice. I have a choice, don't I?

"Hey, Ruby."

Brad?

"Brad! What are you doing here? And in that Neo-Nazi shirt. I'm surprised they let you in — or did you sneak in?"

It's Brad! Grandma, it's Brad! I knew he'd come. Didn't I tell you?

"I've come to see Hil."

"Well, you can just turn around and leave. She doesn't need you now."

No!

"She doesn't look so good. All those tubes, what are they for?"

"Hey, get away! They're keeping her alive. She's dying, for Pete's sake."

I'm alive. Don't listen to her.

"Yeah, I heard."

"How did you hear?"

"The police. They been questioning us. They been asking about the missing kid."

"Yeah, and — ?"

"And nothing. I don't have nothing to say to them."

"What about the accident? Didn't they question you about that?"

"Sure, they been all over me about everything."

"Everything?"

"Yeah, everything. So I'm through talking about it, okay?"

Don't tell her anything, Brad.

"I think I have a right to know what they asked you."

"Hey, it's nothing. Only like if I know anything about some threatening phone calls a bunch of Jews been getting, or about a stack of books on the Holocaust that's disappeared from the library, or about the kid. Things like that."

"Do you? Does Hilary?"

"Hey, they been all over me. I've said nothing. Hear that, Hil? Nothing."

I know. You and me, we stick together. That's what's important, you and me.

"Then what are you so jumpy for? You high? I can tell you, if you looked as nervous and jumpy with the police as you do now, it won't be long before they're arresting you."

"They ain't got nothing on me, lady. Nothing on me 'cause I ain't done nothing. Right, Hil?"

"You talk like she can hear."

"Well, maybe she can. Hilary. Hil, can you hear me?"

"Hey, don't do that. Get away from her. Get your hands off her."

Were you touching me? I want to feel you. I can hear you.

Don't listen to her. Don't let her tell you what to do. She wants me to die.

Brad, when I get well, you and me, let's get married and leave the Warriors. Let's forget about them. We don't need them, or anybody. We can get on the Harley and travel all over the country, and it can be just me and you, together.

"Brad, sit down. Get away from her."

"I'm not hurting her."

"What do you know? She's here because of you. She's dying because of you."

"Listen, I never forced her to get on my bike. What do you think, I did it on purpose? She loved the Harley as much as I did. Said it made her feel alive."

"Sure, look at how alive she's feeling."

Oh, Mama, you don't know. I did feel alive, really alive, riding on his bike. The speed, the air slapping at my face, the smell of the grass and wet trees when we rode over to Burleigh — it was electric. And the freedom, the excitement of getting out on the highway with my arms wrapped around Brad and riding anywhere and nowhere. That was the best part of my life. It's why I'm holding on, why I'm fighting to stay alive. For me and Brad, not you.

"The bike is ruined, anyway."

"Right, Brad, the bike and Hilary, but not you."

"Yeah, not me. Hey, what do you want from me anyway? Want me to lie down on the highway and wait for some Mack truck to flatten me? That ain't gonna do nothing for the Hil girl."

"The least you could do is pretend as if you care."

That's your department, Mother.

"I'm here, ain't I? Look, she knows the score. When you fight for something important, you expect risks. It's no game we're playing here."

"Hey, don't con me. It's all a game. You don't love Hilary. You recruited her the same way they recruited you. The Warriors feed on troubled kids."

"I never told her I loved her. She knows the cause comes first."

But you do love me. Brad, I know you do.

"The cause? You call pestering those Jewish people and destroying their property a cause? You call kidnapping a child a cause? Where is he, Brad? What's happened to the boy?"

Oh, Brad, tell her. Tell someone. Or just go get him yourself. That's it. Get your janitor friend to unlock the school again, and then you can get him out. No one will have to know it was you. Wear your costume. Do it. Then we can forget about this mess and start all over. Get Simon out, Brad. Okay? I never expected it to go this far. I never wanted it to go this far.

Okay, yes, I did. I did. I hated Simon. I hated his stupid beanie, and his schoolbooks carried like silly treasures in his monogrammed backpack, and those squeaky leather shoes. I hated that he enjoyed gardening. I hated hearing his voice through his living room window on those stinkin' summer nights, chanting in some spitty foreign language. And I hated his freakin' happy family where nothing ever went wrong. He wanted me to understand him? Why didn't he ever try to understand me?

"I said, I don't know nothing about that kid."

"And I don't believe you, Brad. What about that note?"

"Lay off me, okay? I didn't come to talk to no dumb-ass mutha, I came to see Hil."

"You watch your language!"

"White Power! Heil, Hitler! Death to Jews, it's the final solution!"

"Keep your voice down. What's wrong with you? You're as jumpy as a . . . Are you on something? Are you high? Do you even know where you are?"

"Yeah, I know where I am. I'm in a friggin' Jew hospital."

"That's enough."

"What? You afraid I might wake Hilary up or something?"

"There is someone else in this room, Brad."

"What? Where? Behind this curtain?"

"Hey! Get away from there and show some respect."

"For that old lady? She's gone already. She ain't hearing nothing."

Oh, Brad, stop. If I could just talk to you. I need to tell you. . . .

"Well, good for you, Brad. Now you've got the nurse coming to the window."

"Look, okay, Ruby. I'm sorry. I ain't out to cause no trouble, really. I just came here to have a word with Hil. In private. Then I'll leave, okay?"

"You can talk, but I'm not leaving. You're too jumpy. I don't like it."

"Hey, listen, Ruby . . ."

"Speak, thus says the Lord:
The dead bodies of men shall fall
like dung upon the open field,
like sheaves after the reaper,
and none shall gather them."

"What's that crap?"

"It's the truth, Brad."

Yes, Mother, it's the truth. My truth.

"It's crap!"

Grandma, I'm tired. My mind, I feel it slipping, I can't hold on. I can't focus. I want to stay with Brad. Why doesn't my mother just go away? Why does she have to stay? If she wants me to die, why does she stay?

Grandma, you're changing. You're like a rainbow. Your hair is blue, and green, and yellow. Your face is red.

I see such pretty colors spinning past me.

I'm spinning, Grandma, spinning away. And the colors, so pretty, so gay . . .

CHAPTER TWELVE

Chana

GAY COLORS CONTINUED to pass before my eyes as my consciousness spun off into this other world. As things began to settle and my eyes began once again to focus, I saw that the colors were from the quilt Mama was tearing. It had belonged to the Krengiels, the only one they had brought with them from Russia. In another time, what Mama was doing would have been a desecration, but these were desperate times, and tearing the quilt so only part of it could be used as a shroud for Mrs. Krengiel's body while the rest was used to keep us warm, that was now just good common sense.

It had been raining, the ground turning to mud, the day Mrs. Krengiel did not go to the straw factory to make the plaits for the inside of the Nazis' army boots. Instead, she dove head-first out our second-story window, broke her neck, and died. Quiet Mrs. Krengiel. Nondescript Mrs. Krengiel, living with us all those months, never sharing her thoughts, never letting her despair show on her face.

I wanted to care about her, about her life, but I was tired of caring. Hers was just one of many bodies found in heaps below second- and third-story windows, or in puddles of blood next to the barbed wire, or in gray decomposing piles waiting to be buried. I feared that if I cared I would be joining them. A soft heart was deadly here in the ghetto.

I saw each day pass much the same as the last: hunger, death, new rules, new jokes, less food, and hot summer nights spent outside in the yard, gathered around the well, talking until dawn. Nothing surprised me anymore, nothing scared me, except deportation orders. Where were they sending those people they rounded up by the hundreds, even thousands, and sent off on the trains? Everyone had their guess, their story to tell, but no one knew for sure. In earlier days the Germans told us that families were being sent to work camps where the living conditions were better. There was more food and less-crowded living space. Postcards even came back from nearby cities, but they all sounded the same and nothing like the friends and relations who sent them.

As time went on, such pretenses were discarded and the Jewish Police would enter homes at night to grab up people who had been selected for deportation and send them off to the central prison. There, they would wait a few torturous days wondering about their fate before being sent off to the trains. Then they were no longer in the hands of the Jewish Police but of the German *Krippo,* who would make them hand over their food, their blankets and backpacks, wedding rings and watches. If they weren't fast enough, they got the whip.

These things we discussed on those moist summer nights in the yard, leaning against the walls of the buildings, against the well, heads turned upward, watching the stars come out. We'd talk and we'd wonder. Where could a body go without his belongings, without his wedding ring and watch? How could these stars and that moon be the same as those that shone elsewhere in the world, and if we were indeed God's *Am S'gulo,* His chosen people, for what exactly had we been chosen?

During the day we would trudge to work (I now worked at the straw factory), and we would watch with dread, our breath held, as the letter carrier passed out his summonses. Would it be our family today? It didn't matter; if it wasn't for us it would surely be for our neighbors or friends.

All this worry and speculation, though, was but a preamble to the nightmare that began on the third anniversary of the war.

I awoke that first morning of September with the sun already burning hot on my face. I sat up, my body feeling beaten from sleeping on the pavement where I had eventually drifted off last night. Anya and her best friend, Hala, still slept soundly beside me. We were used to sleeping outside now, the bedbugs and heat being unbearable inside. Looking beyond the yard I could see Jakub hurrying along, headed this way, and I remembered that not only had he not come home last night, but neither had Bubbe. I searched for Mama in the crowd of bodies propped up against the well and found her slumped against Mrs. Hurwitz, asleep. I ran over to her and shook her awake.

"Mama, Jakub's coming. He looks upset. Maybe it is Bubbe."

Mama and Mrs. Hurwitz sat up, both squinting up at me like sleepy cats. Others stirred around them, shifting their bundles under their heads, trying to find a more comfortable position.

"It is Jakub, see?" I pointed toward him, and Mama, seeing him, rose slowly to her feet, her head wobbling on her neck as though he had delivered a blow to her face.

Jakub stopped a few feet away from her. Panic was in his face, his eyes wide and unblinking.

"Military trucks are pulling up outside the hospital," he said. "They are loading all the sick onto them, tossing them like *treyf*, like unkosher meat, as if they were already dead!"

People jumped up and gathered around him and began

asking questions. Had he seen their brother, or father, or aunt? Where were the people going? What was to be done with them?

Jakub just stared. He couldn't answer them, and he didn't need to. By then, we already knew what was going to happen, where the sick were going. People who had recently entered the ghetto from the provinces had spread the news: Jews shipped out were shipped to their death.

Everywhere was pandemonium as people scooped up their belongings and ran toward the hospital, dropping their sacred soup bowls that went everywhere with them, and not stopping to pick them up. It seemed that in an instant everyone in the ghetto had heard the news. People clogged the streets, rushing to friends or relatives in the hopes of rescuing them, or better, with the hope that perhaps there had been some mistake, that the trucks were just moving them to another building.

I ran with Anya tagging behind me, both of us crying, both of us remembering friends — Mr. Hurwitz, Mrs. Liebman, playmates, workmates — who were in the hospital, but we couldn't get to them. A barricade of Jewish Police blocked off all the streets around the hospital. I could hear shouts and cries and could see patients jumping from windows, trying to escape, but there was nowhere to go.

The next day was more of the same; only, doctors and nurses, the Jewish Police, and even firemen were going to people's houses now. They were examining the elderly and the sick who had tried to hide. Then they were dragging these screaming, pleading people off to the packed buildings to wait for the trucks.

We saw little of Bubbe. She not only had to be present during these examinations, but she made it a point to go around to people's homes afterward and comfort those left behind. Even she couldn't comfort us, however, when Jakub came home and announced that the plan was to make the city of Lodz *judenrein* — Jew clean — the way they had done in Pabianice.

"All of us? We are all to die?" I asked, falling to my knees.

Jakub knelt down next to me, and then Mama and Anya. Together our small family wept and prayed.

I was late for work that day, but it didn't matter. No one was working. We were all talking, tossing around rumors, and scrambling to find jobs for those who had no jobs. Surely they wouldn't take us if we were still of use in the war effort, we reasoned. They needed us. Where else would the Germans get such cheap skilled labor? Mama even went to the school office to register Anya for a real job, waiting in the long lines, baking under the hot summer sun, only to find out that by lunchtime all registrations had become void.

Our workshop closed down at 2:00 that afternoon, and as I walked back toward our home with my friends, I saw men slapping notices on the walls of the buildings. We ran up to one and read that the Chairman was going to speak about the deportation situation in Fireman's Square later that afternoon.

I left my friends and ran home to find my mother, but she wasn't there. All the rooms in our building were deserted. I ran back out into the street and saw that people were already on their way to the square. What else could we do? We could think of nothing else, speak of nothing else, and yet such talk was getting us nowhere. No one had the truth, not even Jakub, and so we waited for hours, crowded in the square, under the boiling sun.

This was our judgment day. It wasn't to take place in the heavens. The good weren't to be saved and the bad banished to hell. Good and bad, sinners and nonsinners — it didn't matter who you were on this judgment day, just how old.

The crowd that had been restless and hot, pushing over to the left side of the yard, trying to find shade, grew silent as the Chairman stepped onto the stage. Chairman Rumkowski. I had seen him many times in the past three years, had listened to many speeches, but never had I seen him look like this, a shriveled-up old man, shoulders slumped, feet dragging — one of us. No good news could come from a man who looked like this.

"A grievous blow has struck the ghetto," he began, his voice trembling. "They are asking us to give up the best we possess — the children and the elderly. I was unworthy of having a child of my own, so I gave the best years of my life to children. I've lived and breathed with children. I never imagined I would be forced to deliver this sacrifice to the altar with my own hands. In my old age I must stretch out my hands and beg: Brothers and sisters, hand them over to me! Fathers and mothers, give me your children!"

He went on and on, but who could hear? All children up to the age of ten were to be simply handed over, surrendered, calmly, orderly — the Germans didn't want any bloodshed. But how could we do it? How could they expect it of us? Did they think because we lived like animals — scavengers in the street, no longer seeing the filth, the blood, the rats — that we'd let them just cart our loved ones off like a loaded barrel of excrement and dump them, dead, somewhere? That was *their* way — the Germans', not ours. They were the heartless beasts, in their fine woolen coats and leather boots made by our hands. We toiled daily in our workshops, starving by their hands, dying, to keep these Germans clothed against the cold. We, the Jews, were the war effort. We were helping them defeat their enemy, and yet their enemy's victory was our only chance for salvation. Could the rest of the world not see the irony? Did they even know? How hard had their hearts become? And God's?

I stood in the square crowded with moaning, whimpering people, people falling to their knees, people fainting, the Chairman's voice pleading, explaining to his microphone, and never had I felt so alone. Where were my mother and grandmother, Jakub and Anya? Where were my friends? Where was God? Couldn't He see that now was the time to save us, before my innocent, my beloved Anya was taken away?

Through the night we listened to the screaming and sobbing of our neighbors. We heard air-raid alarms and bombs dropping, and we whispered prayers for the *Moshiah* to come and save us.

By the next day, most of the moaning and crying had stopped. Now the sounds were muffled and distant, as though someone had tossed a thick woolen blanket over the ghetto.

We spent most of that day out in the streets, restless, wandering, waiting — in silence. The cries and screams went inward, where it was safe, where we could scream and scream and never stop.

When I spoke, I was surprised to hear my voice. It sounded so calm, so normal. Mama's and Bubbe's, too. All of us had gathered together around our table with the two shortened legs, calmly discussing our future as though we were discussing what dress to put on, or how to arrange our hair.

"It is best that we do as the Chairman says and go calmly, Anya and I," Mama said to the rest of us. "If we put up a fight we would only have the *Krippo* knocking us down and shooting us in the back. We have seen how they operate."

Jakub scowled, but even he spoke calmly. "I can hide Anya, Mama. I have places they would never find and the Jewish

Police never search thoroughly. Anya is brave, she could wait this thing out, and I could stay with her."

Bubbe took his hand. "Jakub, I have gone the rounds with the doctors, watched them select the elderly for deportation; they have a quota they have to fill. If they do not get who they are after, the police will just put someone else in her place."

"So, that is good. Anya will be safe," Jakub replied.

Bubbe squeezed his hand. He looked down at the table, pressing his finger on a hardened crumb of bread he had spotted and touching it to his tongue.

Mrs. Hurwitz, who had spent the past two days making futile efforts to get her husband out of the group already selected for deportation, had joined us. We were her only family now. She looked around at all of us and then pulled Anya up onto her lap. "I will go with Anya, or even instead of Anya, if we can figure out how. Maybe I can be with my husband then." She kissed the back of Anya's head.

"I know a place where we can all hide," I said, remembering those peaceful afternoons I spent listening to the orchestra from the hole in the ceiling of the House of Culture. I explained it to them. How there was enough room for everyone, how we could hide there for days if we had to.

Everyone listened, especially Jakub and Anya. Will it really work? How big is the hole? How big is the space above the hole? Is it dark? Could we hide in the corners behind the rafters? Should we try it? Do we dare?

No one was capable of making this decision. Round and round we went. I could see that Jakub was enthusiastic about the idea, but he wasn't going to be the one to press us into action. The burden of guilt he carried around after the death of the two brothers still weighed heavily upon him.

Bubbe, too, was hesitant, believing now more than ever

that it was best just to let life unfold and not get in one's own way with so much plotting and planning, to leave it all in God's hands.

Mrs. Hurwitz felt her plan, to go on the truck instead of Anya, was the best one, and whether we hid or not, she would stay and let fate run its course.

Mama just didn't know. "Should we hide, only to be discovered and shot on the spot, or take a chance on the trucks? Would our fate be any different either way?" she asked.

We had so little time to make up our minds, and as events closed in on us, the decision seemed impossible to make. Hunger, fear, outrage, all made it hard to think clearly, to be certain we were even making sense. The workshops and the soup kitchens were closed. There was almost no food to be had anywhere, and by late afternoon new notices had been posted. Beginning at 5:00 P.M. there was to be a general *szpera*, a curfew, until further notice. If we were going to hide, we would have to get out right away, before the curfew. We would have to hurry through the streets to our new home, a hole in the ceiling, and stay hidden for who knew how many days without food or water, sweltering in the attic heat.

It was Anya who finally helped us make up our minds. She had slid down off Mrs. Hurwitz's lap and now stood behind Mama, her arms wrapped around Mama's shoulders, her head resting on her own arms.

"Mama, I am tired," she said. "Are you not tired, too? Can we just lie down together?" She lifted her head and squeezed Mama's shoulders. "I want to do that more than anything in the world, just lie down with you."

We didn't hide. We slept, we prayed, we worried, and we watched through our window, that night and all through the next day. We also starved. There was nothing to eat, and we realized that if this kept up much longer, they wouldn't need to deport us, they could just drag us all to the cemetery.

The evening of that third night, we gathered around the table again. Already the Jewish Police had raided the old-age home on Dworska Street and had gone to Rybna Street, to people's homes, and had torn the children out of their mothers' arms. The news had spread in hushed desperate tones like the leaves sweeping through the streets, and we knew that in the next day or two, it would be our turn.

As I looked around the table at Jakub, my mother and grandmother, Mrs. Hurwitz and Anya, I saw that we had all changed in the last two days. It wasn't just the hollowing of our cheeks and the ashen color of our skin, it was also our attitude. We had each reached a certain peace within ourselves, a certain understanding of how it was going to be, and, yes, a certain acceptance. Perhaps it was Bubbe's words drummed into our heads all these years about trusting in God, knowing where to put one's faith, waiting and hoping — always hoping. Perhaps, too, we were just following Jewish tradition — having inherited thousands of years of suffering and persecution, we had learned how to adapt and accept, and believe that through our strength and our faith, we would survive. Or perhaps we were all going insane. Maybe this was some middle stage of insanity, this peace and acceptance a self-deception. Maybe in a day or two we'd run screaming through the streets, but for now it was enough to gather around the table and hold hands, and perhaps for the last time, share our thoughts.

"I do not know how it will be these next few days. We have no control over any of the things going on around us," Mama said, looking pointedly at Jakub and me. "So much have they taken from us already, but what is inside us, they can never take away, unless we let them, unless we give it away.

"I go out into the streets and see the guards on the other side of the fence mocking us, laughing at us with their warm coats and overfed bodies, but I laugh at them. I pity them, those beasts. They think that by taking away our homes, our rights, and by starving us, they have taken everything and we are nothing, less than the rats and the lice that feed on us. They do not see that it is they who are nothing. They are hardened layers of skin, and what is beneath that skin? Nothing. They have lost it all. All that will ever matter, they have lost. And I laugh at them, and mock them, because they do not even know it."

"Yes, but Mama, I want them to know it," Anya said.

"Then be brave and hold your head up high. Do not let them get inside you."

Jakub shook his head. "If you hold up your head you have just given them a better target to shoot."

"Jakub, if I am to die at their hands, I want to make sure it gives them no satisfaction. I want the memory of my face, my eyes, to burn on their souls forever."

Jakub laughed. "You forget, Mama, they have no souls."

We all laughed.

Then Mama got serious again.

"Anya and I will go together when the time comes, and Jakub, Chana, you will remain here with Bubbe and do as she says. And please, when this is all over, find Nadzia. Let her know how we loved her."

"But, Mama!" I began to cry.

"I cannot send her off on her own," Mama said, as she rubbed my back.

"I know, but it is not fair." I looked up. "I am going, too. I want to go with you. How can I let you go and never know what happened to you?"

"No, Chana. You are sixteen years old now. That's old enough to understand what is happening. I must ask you to stay here with Bubbe. You must honor this last request."

I hung my head and didn't say anything. What was I going to do without Mama and Anya? With Bubbe always so busy at the hospital and Jakub busy with his underground work, I had come to rely on Mama and Anya; they were my best friends.

It must have been no later than six o'clock the next morning when we heard a round of gunshots in the courtyard below and a harsh German voice shout, *"Alles raus!* — Everybody out!"

We scrambled to our feet and hurried to the stairs. We could hear the wagons rolling into the yard. We knew instantly what had happened. The Jewish Police hadn't done a thorough enough job of rounding us up and so the Germans had taken over. There would be no chance for pleading now.

We raced out into the yard and stood erect and still, waiting for others to hobble over the stones on weak and swollen legs and join the line.

I saw Mr. Eliasberg stumble out. He was old and weak, looking dazed from being awakened from a deep sleep. His thin gray hair was standing straight up on his head. He tried to hurry out to the yard, but someone brushed too close to him and knocked him down. He struggled to get back up, but before he could even get to his hands and knees, they shot him.

Good-bye to Mr. Eliasberg. Do not look at him. Do not think about him. Harden your heart. Remember, the softhearted do not survive. The softhearted do not survive! Good-bye, clumsy, silly Mr. Eliasberg.

The Germans fired more shots as mothers wailed and pleaded, as children were discovered hidden in barrels and closets, as latecomers made their way across the yard, their treasures loaded onto their backs. The message was clear: Do only as they say, exactly as they say, or your yellow, bilious blood will be all that runs over these stones.

Poor Anya tried to stand tall, her eyes like two black stones staring out from sockets too large for her head. She wanted to appear older that she was, but her body was too thin, too frail, too tiny. She still looked six years old, but she held her head high and I knew, despite her appearance, there stood a child with the wisdom of an old woman and a heart so big and soft it had cushioned the blows of the ghetto for all of us.

A gloved hand came down on her shoulder and yanked her from the line, and Mama, who had been holding on tightly to Anya's left hand, came flying out with her, almost knocking over the *Krippo*. He was young, maybe eighteen or nineteen, and his rosy, blue-eyed face bore such an expression of hatred I thought he would shoot them both right there before my eyes. Had Bubbe not been holding onto me, I would have flung myself onto the man, and with any luck, at least have scraped off the crazy smile frozen like winter on his face.

Two Jewish Police came up behind the *Krippo* and grabbed Mama and Anya and tossed them onto the wagon before the *Krippo* could decide whether to shoot or toss. It was all that they could do now, and perhaps it was futile, this attempt to prevent more bloodshed. They were merely delaying the inevitable, weren't they? I was grateful to them just the same.

Mrs. Hurwitz now stood to my right, filling in the space that Mama and Anya had left. Her body was bent forward, her head flopped onto her chest, and as I stared at this woman who had aged maybe twenty years in the past week, I could not believe that she was the same woman who worked by my side, her thick strong arms scrubbing back and forth on the stairs, just a few years ago. I had wanted to be like her, but now I saw her strength was only muscular and easily stripped away by starvation.

Of course they pulled her out of the line and tossed her onto the wagon, the silly fool. If they hadn't, I think I would have. Her they could have; just give me back Mama and Anya.

I looked over at the wagon already overflowing with arms and legs. It was ready to pull out. Mama and Anya stood up and blew final kisses. I tried to blow some back, but my mouth had frozen into some horrible contortion that I could see mirrored on the faces of others, like me, who were left behind. It was a wild look, our mouths open and drawn back across our faces, our cries, our screams, no more than air escaping from our lungs, soundlessly bellowed across the yard.

As the wagon began to jerk forward and move out toward the street, I saw Mrs. Hurwitz rise up from the heap, and with her head held as high and proud as Mama's and Anya's, she waved to me. She had gotten what she wanted. Then the three of them turned away from us and linked arms. They were ready.

I didn't need my secret friend, with the face that had peered so knowingly at me every time I faced death in some way, to whisper to me that they would be all right. That the Germans, no matter what they chose to do with them, would never defeat them, I already knew. Still, she came, and that was a comfort.

CHAPTER THIRTEEN

Hilary

I CAN'T SEE.

It doesn't matter. I don't want to see, or hear. I'm all alone here.

I'm so cold.

"Hil? Hil, it's me. It's Brad. I probably don't have much time. Your mother just went to get some coffee. She's crazy, you know that?"

Please, I want Mama. I want Anya back. How can they just do that? How can they just take them and treat them like—like . . .

"Things are good. We've got some more people, more warriors, and that other girl—that Megan O'Toole. Remember her?"

They should have taken me, not Anya. She was so good. She was always so cheerful, full of life. What am I? I'm a burden. I'm a burden to Bubbe and Jakub.

"There's a parade next week down in Washington, D.C., and a bunch of us are going. We'll show them how big we are. We're going to march in full uniform. We've got those leaflets, too, and we're going to drop them out of a window somewhere. It's big, Hil, like we wanted, remember? They'll be coming from all over the U.S."

She always had extra food for me. Why would God take

her? She was the strong one. And Mama, so good. I need her. I need them. Doesn't God see? Doesn't He know?

God, listen to me.

"The police, they're on our backs, they're on us all the time, and they don't see we're doing them a favor. Hey, we're just getting rid of all the undesirable elements. Right, babe? The Jew lovers."

God, it should have been me. Why didn't I volunteer to go on that truck? Why did I hold back? How could I have let Mama and Anya just go? Where are they? God?

"That Megan, the new girl, she's one violent piece of work. Tiny, like you, but all fire. Pure hate, you know? She's here, now, in this building. I—I said it was all right if she wore your jacket. You left it down in the meeting room. It's a good thing, huh, or it would have gotten all tore up in the wreck. You wouldn't want my birthday present to you in shreds. She's taking good care of it. It fits her."

Could I pray? Would that help?

"Hey, two Jews were shot a couple of nights ago. That's good, huh? It was one of us, but I don't know who. No one's saying. They'll be all over me again, now that they got my name. Hey, who cares, right. For the cause. Heil, Hitler, man. It's worth it to go to jail, but if I go, I'm going to take a Jew out first, even if it's just a little Jew, a little Simon Jew. It's one less, right? Yeah, if I'm going to jail, I'm going to make sure I did something worth going for."

Our Father who art in heaven, hallowed be Thy name. Thy kingdom come, Thy will be done, on earth as it is in heaven. . . .

"Things are heating up, Hil. That's a pun, in case you didn't know. Right now, while I'm talking, things are heating up. Megan's down in one of them ladies' rooms setting up the fireworks. This whole building's going to go up in flames.

You're a hero, Hil. Remember that. You're dying for the cause. White Power!"

Give us this day our daily bread; and forgive us our debts, as we also have forgiven our debtors; and lead us not into temptation, but deliver us from evil.

Yes. Deliver us from evil. Dear God, deliver us from evil.

"Hil, I've got to go. I can hear your mother coming. How does she walk in those pointy-heeled slipper things she wears? She's crazy. Heil, Hitler, babe. See you in hell."

CHAPTER FOURTEEN

Chana

"BUBBE, why are we still here?" I heard myself asking as I sat in the dark, huddled on the floor, my throbbing head resting against a strange wall.

"Because God wills it," Bubbe murmured, her voice not needing to travel far to be heard. "And because we must be the ones to remember, and carry on, for future generations."

"Phfutt." I spit, ignoring that she was not answering my question about the prison, but her own about life and still being alive. "What generations? They are gone. So many people. So many deaths. How could God allow it? Bubbe?"

"Yes, Chana."

"I don't think there is a God."

"Perhaps not your God."

"Will He strike me down for not believing?"

Bubbe chuckled.

"I would not care if He did. At least there would be a reason for it. I think that is what I understand the least, this useless, pointless suffering and dying. Why do they not just shoot us and get it over with anyway?"

I heard the stranger on the other side of me draw in her breath and begin to recite the *Shema Yisrael.*

"Hush, Chana! You are frightening the others," Bubbe hissed.

I looked around me, trying to see the shapes of the faces that stared back at me through the darkness. Who were they? What were their crimes? Were they like Bubbe and me? Had they escaped from some ghetto only to be caught and thrown into prison? Had they been tortured as we had been? Had they planned their defense as Bubbe and I had done, so we were sure to give the same explanation for our presence on the train where we were caught?

I closed my eyes and wondered how long we had been there. It seemed weeks since we had last had something to eat or drink, but I supposed it must have been only a few days. What did it really matter? Starving was starving; thirst was thirst.

During the hours when the Nazis left us alone in our cell with the others, I liked to close my eyes and remember the night before we were caught. Never had I felt as victorious as I did that night, standing with Bubbe beneath the warm glow of an electric light, in a house with running water, a toilet, and heat, and staring up into the friendly yet disguised faces of our rescuers.

Thanks to Jakub our escape had been easy. A few planks against the wall beyond the cemetery, set up at just the right place and just the right time, and we were up and over the wall and fleeing into the night. There were no gunshots or whistles or dogs behind us. Everything was timed perfectly. I could just feel it inside that everything was going to work. I felt no panic as we scurried through the forbidden alleys in the new leather shoes that Jakub had somehow procured, and our somewhat new coats without the Star of David stitched to their fronts and backs. I said a quick prayer as I followed my grandmother into the backseat of a car that had a doll lying beneath the back window. I hoped we hadn't somehow chosen the wrong car.

As we settled in, the man turned around in his seat and I saw the fuzziest face I had ever seen. He was all beard and mustache and eyebrows. The only other things that stood out were his ears. He spoke to us in German and for a moment I thought we had indeed climbed into the wrong car. I felt my whole body go limp, like a puppet cut loose from its strings. I saw Bubbe smile and heard her respond also in German, and although I understood the language quite well, I didn't hear a word they said. The man handed us each a blindfold and Bubbe explained to me in my dumbfounded stupor that we were to wear them so we would be unable to tell anyone where we had been should we ever get caught.

"*Ja, ja!*" The man nodded. Then he turned back around and sped off through the alley. We didn't speak the rest of the trip.

I tried to settle back in my seat as we passed through what must have been familiar towns, but I found that my body was shaking, my teeth chattering. Bubbe reached out for my hand and squeezed it. I tried to smile and then realized she couldn't see me. I took a deep breath and snuggled up against her. I felt guilty that she had to keep reassuring me, to keep comforting me. After all, I was the reason we were here. I was the reason we were risking our lives. I was the one who had to leave. I couldn't stay there in the ghetto, not without Mama and Anya. It was too much to ask. I had tried. After the end of the roundup of the children and the elderly and the infirm, we were all supposed to go back to work, to get on with our lives — but how could I, when all that was my life was gone?

Every day I dreamed of running away, of hiding, of curling up into a ball in a hole somewhere and just staying there until

I died. It's what I wanted to do, but Bubbe wouldn't let me. She kept me busy — hop, hop, hop — every day. She had me running errands, standing in long lines for our food rations, going with her as she went around to visit the sick who refused to go to the hospital, returning to my own job at the workshop, and preparing the nightly soups. Yes, she kept me busy, but not so busy that I didn't notice a child here and there hurrying along the streets, or trying to sell the last stale bits of homemade sweets. And why were they still in the ghetto and Anya and Mama gone? Were they special? Were they the privileged ones, children of the Jewish Police, perhaps? It wasn't fair. I couldn't stand to see them.

Nothing, though, was as unbearable as when a new family moved into our one-room home. All of them were still to-gether — mother, father, and three children. It was too much. I had been preparing the evening meal when the five of them walked in, all smiles, their arms full of bundles that they dropped at their feet as soon as they had entered.

"Yes, it is true," the father said, acknowledging my aston-ishment, "we are to live here with you. It is just you?"

I could not help hearing the hopefulness in his voice. The two girls, mop-headed twins, were already laying claim to one of the cots as they shook off their shoes and climbed in.

"No," I said. "My bubbe and Jakub, my brother, are with me. My sister and mother were taken in the roundup last September."

"And now it is almost Chanukah. We will be celebrating together," the father said as if he had not heard me.

I placed the wooden spoon I was holding down on the table and picked up my coat from the chair. Then, after smiling at the mother, father, and son — who were still standing like straw-stuffed dummies amongst their belongings — I left.

It wasn't until I reached the street that I began to run and to let myself cry. I ran through the dark streets still crowded with people dragging home from their jobs, hopping over people lying along the curbs, too cold, too starved to move. I didn't know where I was running until I was there — at the House of Culture. Yes, I thought to myself as I faced the building with its roof still shining green, even in the dark. I will hide up there in my special place, and I will never come out. I will die up there. I will die and they will play the most beautiful music in the world in the concert hall beneath me. A wonderful way to die.

As I entered the building I could hear voices in the distance and the sounds of various instruments tuning up. I waited a moment and listened for the violins. I wished that I had brought my violin with me. I didn't want to play it, I just wanted it with me. It was a beautiful instrument — my father had had it made especially for me for my tenth birthday — and the thought of those two little girls back in the room finding it and putting their dirty hands all over it almost made me turn back — but no, I had come here to die. I wouldn't need my violin in heaven. I crept down the hallway and into the side room and looked up at the ceiling. The hole had been sealed up.

I could see the board by the light in the hallway, but I didn't understand. It can't be sealed, I told myself. I climbed onto the door handle and then clung onto the top of the door with one hand as I pressed against the board. Surely it would give way. This was my special place. They can't take away my special place. I pushed and banged as I wobbled and swung on the door. "No!" I shouted, and banged some more.

"No, child, you must get down from there."

I felt someone grab me from behind and lower me down

from the door. I flopped out of his arms and sank all the way down onto the floor and hid my crying face in my skirt.

"You do not want to be going up there" came a man's gentle voice.

"What do you know about it?" I sobbed.

"I know it has not been cleaned. They just sealed it up. Was it your family they shot up there? Is there something up there, perhaps, that you feel they may have left behind for you?"

I looked up at the man, seeing him for the first time. His skin was gray, his cheekbones sharp ridges cutting into his flesh, but his eyes, even in the dimness of the light, drew me toward him. I knew, like me, he had lost. He held out his hand to me and I took it. He smiled. Maybe everything would be all right. Starvation and loss had not cut off all feelings. This man was reaching out to me, and together, for a little while perhaps, we could be father and daughter.

I stood up and looked again at the sealed-up hole.

"How is it that you were not up there with them?" the man asked, still holding my hand.

I stared at him, my mouth open, but I could make no sound come out.

"A nightmare, those days. I lost so many — and you, your whole family. Such evil cannot last forever."

"My whole family," I repeated. "No, not my whole family, just — just my mother and sister, I . . ." I could not go on. At last I understood. I looked back up at the ceiling and I saw the hole again, but this time it was as if the board was not covering it. I could see sunlight shining through it, and then beyond the hole at the back of the attic, a family huddled — watching the German Police approach — blankets, photographs, clothing collected at their feet. I saw the Nazis' eyes, as cold and dark and soulless as the revolver aimed at the faces of the family. I saw the blood. I felt it dripping onto my face, and I pulled away from beneath the hole, out of reach of the man's hands. What was I doing here? What silly notion had I had to think that I was going to lie up there and drift blissfully off to heaven while a Bach concerto echoed in the rooms below? Death was ugly. Hadn't I seen enough of it to know at least that?

The man took a step forward. I backed away, his eyes no longer able to keep me there.

"I should not have spoken of your family." He pointed toward the ceiling.

"They were not my family. They were *not* my family," I shouted. "It has nothing to do with me! They are nothing — nothing to me!"

I ran from the man with the caring eyes, and he did not call me back. I knew of no place else to go, and so I ran back home, back to the room with the five strangers — three of them children under ten.

It would have been unbearable had I not decided to escape. Day and night from that day forward I plotted my escape route, watching where and when others from my side of the fence stole their way to the Aryan side in search of food or work. So many people were willing to risk their lives this way, and yet just living in the ghetto was a risk to one's life. To survive was to be at risk.

Whenever I was with Bubbe, however, I made it a point to be thinking of anything but my plans of escape. I didn't want her figuring out my plans and trying to stop me.

One evening in early January, as we were returning home from our visits with the homebound patients, Bubbe said to me, "You are happier now, Chana? You are doing better?"

I turned my head away from the fence, away from the icicles

that wrapped around the barbed wire and gleamed, beckoning, whispering, willing me to go and touch. "Yes, I am doing better, but I still miss Mama and Anya."

Bubbe nodded. "You think they are out there somewhere."

I jerked my head up and looked into her eyes. What was the use of pretending with Bubbe? I tucked my chin into the collar of my coat. "Yes," I said.

"Then we must look for them." Bubbe took my hand. "I will get Jakub to plan our escape."

"You what? Bubbe!" I threw my arms around her and squeezed. "You knew all along." I stepped back and stared at the face of my amazing bubbe. "Is it true? Will you go with me?"

"You must promise me one thing."

I spread out my arms and spun around. "Anything!"

"We will do it Jakub's way. We will leave when he says it is all right. You must be patient."

"Yes! Yes! Yes! I promise."

It was March before Jakub could arrange things on the outside and gather the shoes and clothing appropriate for a grand-mother and granddaughter traveling through Poland. We had known Jakub would not want to go with us. He had his own life now, one of which I knew Mama and Tata and even Zayde would be proud. Still, as the night of our escape approached, the idea of leaving him behind, of saying good-bye to yet another member of the family, became unbearable, and I begged Jakub to go with us.

"No, it is too late to be changing plans," Jakub told me in a voice that had recently become deeper, richer—his adult voice. "If this is to work, you must not be thinking about me.

You are moving away, forward, into the Aryan world, and all your attention must be focused there. It is your *life*, Chana."

"Yes, but I need—"

"You are not serious about leaving then. I have made all these plans. Henrick will be waiting. For nothing I have made these plans?"

"No, Jakub, I am going. But I will miss you. Can you let me at least say that?"

"There will be no time to spend missing me. We will see each other again. Keep that in your mind. We will stand together at Hitler's execution."

"Oh, Jakub, do you think it will ever happen? Will this ever be over?"

Jakub moved forward in his chair and grabbed my hand. He lowered his voice. "I have learned that the German Sixth Army has surrendered to Russia."

"What? When? Where? Oh, Jakub, really?"

He nodded. "February second, in Stalingrad. Seems the winters are a bit too hard for the Germans. You will see, before the end of 1943 this war will be over."

I grabbed Jakub around the neck and hugged him. "And we'll all be together—you, me, Bubbe, Mama, Anya, and Nadzia. Oh, what a celebration!"

"Chana, you must listen. We need to keep our minds on the plans. Now, tell me again what you are to do."

"Bubbe knows the plans. You know I will be safe with Bubbe. She won't forget."

"Chana! You are being foolish and unrealistic. You could be separated or Bubbe could get—killed. It could happen, you know it could."

"I am to get into the car that is waiting in the alley. There will be a doll with a missing foot lying in the back window.

We will get in and Henrick — not his real name — will take us to a house where he will take our pictures and give us papers that say that we are Rachela and Ewa Krisowski. Then we are to get ourselves into the roundup of Polish workers going to Germany, which you say is easy to do because of all the chaos, but we will see. Then we will ride to Germany — *phfutt* — where our false papers will be less suspicious since all the Jews have been rounded up there already, and we will work beside the Germans — *phfutt*. There now, did I leave anything out?"

On the night of our escape the air was cold and dry, the night sky clear and alive with the stars and the moon. It was unusual weather for that time of the year. We had counted on the damp and the fog to keep us under cover as we hurried through the alleys to the waiting car. Just the same, I preferred the clear night. It made me feel awake, electric, invincible. Once inside the car, riding with the blindfold on, that charge, that energy, left me, and all I could do was fold myself up against Bubbe and cry. It was too much for me to believe we were free.

The car stopped and we removed our blindfolds. We were parked outside a freshly painted farmhouse, glowing white beneath the moon. We got out of the car and Henrick led us inside. His wife, Lili, showed us the bathroom with its running water, and our bedroom, with two heavy blankets folded at the bottom of the bed. We took off our coats and left them in the bedroom and then followed Lili into the kitchen. She handed each of us a plate of eggs, cheese, warm fresh bread, and whole boiled potatoes.

After supper, we each took a hot bath and climbed into bed, sinking into a soft pillow of eiderdown. Then Lili gave us the two bricks she had warmed by the kitchen fire, and we tucked them under the blankets, down by our feet. I snuggled up to Bubbe and sighed. "If only every day from now on could be this wonderful," I whispered.

I had dreamed of waking up to the smell of eggs, sausage, and coffee so many times in the past few years that when I awoke that next morning I thought I was dreaming once again. I kept my eyes closed and let the warmth of that room, with the sun streaming in from behind me and spreading out over my bed, melt me deeper into the pillow, the eiderdown, the bed. This is what it's like to feel rich, I told myself. It's all I need. I will never open my eyes and everything will stay as it is this very moment.

I felt a hand on my shoulder and heard Bubbe whisper that it was time to get up, but I couldn't open my eyes. It was too real, this warmth, the richness, the deep comfort. Hang on to it, I told myself, hang on.

"Chana, we must begin. You will want breakfast before we leave."

I clutched the blanket, already pulled up around my ears — hang on.

"We must return to Lodz this morning." Bubbe shook my shoulder.

The nightmare, it's intruding on my beautiful dream — hold on tighter, hold on.

"Chana, now you must get up. There has been a roundup this morning. We will have to hurry."

A roundup. The old nightmare was moving in. Was this Tata's roundup, where they dragged him out of his own house and made him shovel dirt and shot him in a tree? Or was it Zayde's, where they drove us out of our homes and into the ghetto and worked him to death? Or maybe it was Mama's and Anya's roundup, where they used guns and dogs and whips to drive them into the carts and haul them away. Smell the sausage, thick, rich . . .

"Chana!"

"Bubbe, please."

"More tears? This has been too much for you. I will let you decide. We can go back to Lodz to the ghetto or we can go to Lodz and join the roundup — but, Chana, we cannot stay here. It is too dangerous."

I wiped my face and sat up. "A roundup. How could any good come from that?"

"For freedom, we will have to take our chances."

"But joining the workers and going to Germany, how will we find Mama and Anya that way? It would be better to live and hide in the *puszcza*, the forest."

"You promised you would do as Jakub said. In the forest we would not survive long. We must first be safe before we can find out about your mother and Anya. We must trust Jakub, Chana. He said this plan is good. He said it has worked before." Bubbe pulled back the covers. "Now, quickly get dressed. I have here all your papers, your passport, birth certificate, your ration card, everything. We will tuck them in your coat, Ewa."

I smiled. "Yes, Rachela." I threw on my skirt and blouse and then sat on the edge of the bed to wipe last night's dust off my new shoes with the edge of my skirt. As I polished them, I watched Bubbe collect the few belongings we had brought with us. All I brought was my violin. It wasn't practical, as Jakub had pointed out to me several times, but it was all I wanted.

"Bubbe, is what we are doing a sin?" I asked her when she came back over to the bed and sat next to me. "Won't God punish us for pretending to be Ewa and Rachela, non-Jews?"

"We are saving our lives and harming no one. It is more important, I think, to behave as God's chosen people, in the way of the covenant, than to proclaim we are His chosen people. You understand, Chana?"

"I think so. Although we say we are two Catholic women from Lodz, Ewa and Rachela, we will always behave and believe as Jews."

"It will not be forever. Now you go eat yourself a good breakfast. You will get fat this morning, eh?"

As Jakub had said, becoming part of the roundup of Polish workers was easy. There was chaos everywhere. Armed guards were posted in front of roadblocks, and packed behind them were the people they had rounded up from a local church. People were so busy shouting across the barricade to their friends and relatives, pleading with the deaf guards, saying good-bye to loved ones, trying to slip out from behind the blocks and join the throngs in the street, that no one bothered with the two of us as we strolled down the street toward the assembly and slipped past the barricades. The guards had no objection to people wanting to get in, just out.

When the train arrived, the guards separated the men and women and loaded us into separate cars. There was more chaos as husbands and wives tried to stay together while guards pushed and pulled and beat the people into the train.

Bubbe and I said nothing to one another or to anyone else. We pushed our way to the back of the car and sat down. I held onto Bubbe's hand and watched as other women, many in tears, tried to find a seat. Finally the train lurched forward. Bubbe squeezed my hand and whispered, "Freedom."

We had been riding for perhaps an hour and a half—I with my head resting on Bubbe's shoulder—when I felt Bubbe squeeze my hand again. I knew that this time she was signaling not pleasure but danger. I opened my eyes and standing before me was an old schoolmate, Marila Yankowitz, as fat and hairy as ever.

Her eyes widened as I looked up at her. She pointed a stubby finger at me and said in a booming voice, "Yes, I thought so. I know you!"

CHAPTER FIFTEEN

Chana

I TRIED NOT TO BE BITTER about Marila turning us over to the Germans. As Bubbe had said, she had been separated from her family, and it was her chance to get back home. When the guards tossed us out of the train, however, and we landed on our knees on the concrete, I couldn't help but wish I could shove Marila under a moving train.

Two other guards, ones I hadn't seen before, ordered us to get up and come with them. They led us out of the train station and through the gray, unlit streets of a bustling German town. The people on the sidewalks were hurrying home for supper, but all of them took a little time to stop and watch the guards march us along, guns at our shoulders.

I wondered where they were taking us. Were they going to shoot us? Was this the last I'd see of the world? We stopped in front of a well-lit building with iron gates that towered above our heads. More guards were waiting for us there. They took us inside, led us down a long corridor and into a dingy, foul-smelling shower room. Here two women washed us in disin-fectant, cut our hair—no style, just chop, chop—and handed us prison clothes. I watched them as they hauled away my clothes, my coat, and my violin.

My violin! Would I ever see it again? Would I ever play it again? Did orchestras still exist on the outside, or had they disappeared with the war, with Hitler and his mission of hatred and annihilation? Were they now just echoes from within the ghetto, echoes of a time and a world that could never be again?

A Defense Corps wardress with a beautiful face and deep creases in her forehead led us to another room and took our fingerprints and our pictures. Then she marched us downstairs through yet another corridor, this one lined on both sides with narrow cells. She opened the door to one of the cells and motioned for Bubbe to enter. Bubbe squeezed my hand and murmured, "Have cheer, at least we were not shot." Then she stepped past the wardress, bowed, and said, "*Danke*," and the door closed behind her.

I followed the wardress down to the end of the hall, up a short set of stairs, and into a large room. The first thing I saw upon entering the room was my violin case. Without thinking I made a move toward it and two men, the wardress, and another woman charged toward me.

"My violin," I said as I backed away from them.

One of the men, a tall, emaciated-looking man with a fat nose and glasses that sat smashed up against his face, grinned down at me.

"You want your violin?" he asked me in German.

"*Jawohl*," I replied. Of course I did.

"Good, we can arrange that for you. If you tell us your name and where you got these papers"—he gestured to my passport and birth certificate on the desk behind him—"then you will get your violin back and everyone will be happy. It is easy, no?"

I opened my mouth to speak and saw the other woman in the room hurry to her typewriter, which sat on a small desk at the right-hand side of the room. She was almost a midget, coming up to, perhaps, my rib cage, and yet her hands were normal-sized, with long, thick fingers that waited poised above the typewriter for me to speak.

"My name is Ewa Krisowski," I said. "That is all I have ever been called. If I have another name, I do not know it."

The man snapped his fingers. "Give me that paper with the names on it."

One of the other men, also tall, but well-filled out, lunged toward the larger desk in the center of the room and grabbed up a sheet of paper. He handed it to the man with the fat nose.

"You are Chana Shayevitsh, are you not? A Jew from Lodz, Poland."

"That girl from the train must have told you that. She wanted very badly to return to Poland. Of course, she told you that so she could be set free. I, too, have family I left behind. They do not know where I am. She was clever, that girl from the train. She fooled everyone. Even you."

The man with the fat nose straightened up. His eyes darted sideways to the other man beside him and then returned to me. In less than a second his expression changed from pleasant but serious to ragingly angry as his skeletal hand came down upon my shoulder in a chop that knocked me to my knees. It felt as if my collarbone had snapped in two. Where had his strength come from?

I began to stand up, but again his hand came down upon the same shoulder and rammed me back on the floor. I stayed there, frozen, my left shoulder throbbing.

"Now you understand. To enter the *Reich* illegally is a serious crime. You will tell me where you got those papers."

"I have always had them. I do not know what more I can say." I braced myself for another blow but none came. Instead he ordered the wardress to take me away so I could think about it awhile.

As I stood up to leave, I saw through the window that dawn was breaking and wondered if the Germans ever slept.

The wardress took me back to the cells and opened the one where Bubbe was waiting. When she saw me, her eyes filled with tears and she reached out for my hands.

Before I could respond, the wardress had stepped in and grabbed Bubbe's arm. She pulled her out of the cell. I wanted her to know that I hadn't said anything.

"Good-bye, Rachela," I said.

I don't know how long I had slept but when I awoke Bubbe had still not returned. I stood up and peered through the door. I hadn't noticed earlier if there were any other prisoners in this hall of cells, but now I could hear movement coming from the cell next door.

"Rachela?" I called out. "Rachela, is that you?"

I heard a low chuckle coming from the cell to my right. "She'll not be coming back, that one," a voice muttered.

I backed away from the door as though it were a wall of fire. What does she know? She doesn't know.

"Please, Bubbe, please come back."

I waited — hours? days? I didn't know. The lighting in the windowless cells never changed. All I knew was that Bubbe was not with me and that I was so thirsty I had begun to lick the bars on my door as if they were bars of ice. I had not been fed or given anything to drink since we had arrived. I thought perhaps I would go mad. I slept as much as I could, always hopeful that when I awoke Bubbe would be standing in front of me, her hand reaching down to pat my head.

Every time I heard the light steps of the wardress tapping

down the hall, I rushed to the door, expecting to see Bubbe behind her, but she was never there.

I prayed for long periods of time, stringing together any bits of prayer I could remember.

"Look upon us in our suffering and fight our struggles," I prayed, recalling the seventh blessing of the *Shemoneh Esrei.* "Redeem us speedily, for Thy name's sake, for Thou art a mighty Redeemer. Blessed art Thou, Lord, Redeemer of Israel."

I repeated this for hours and tried to convince myself that Bubbe was all right, that she was alive. I was down on my knees chanting with my eyes closed when I felt a presence in the room. I turned toward the door, expecting to see Bubbe, but instead I saw my "friend," the one I had seen before the death of my father, and before we left for the ghetto, and then again as Mama and Anya were carted away.

"You have been a comfort to me before," I said to the image before me, as though she were real, "but not now. You are always here when someone leaves me. You bring with you bad news. Go away."

I closed my eyes and began reciting my prayers, but I could tell she was still behind me. Finally, I could take it no longer. I whipped around and shouted, "What have you to tell me then? Bubbe is dead? I know that! Now you can leave. Go away and never return, never! There is no one left. There is no reason for you ever to come back. I'm all alone. I'm all alone!"

I crawled up onto the bed and cried, my face buried in the mattress. I was going mad, hallucinating. I could feel my insides boiling up in my throat. I cried harder, trying to block out the presence of that girl. I could feel her drawing closer, feel her standing right next to the bed. I looked up at her and stopped crying. I felt something cold and heavy run through me like an iron, smoothing out all the black knots inside of me. My breathing slowed down until I was hardly breathing at all. I lay on my back with my eyes closed and felt the stale air inside the cell evaporate, leaving behind fresh air and the scent of grass.

"Thank you," I whispered. "I am all right now." I opened my eyes and smiled at her. "Thank you, my *shvester*. I — I will call you that, *Shvester*, because sisters have a special bond."

A few minutes later I heard the jangle of keys outside my door. I sat up and saw the wardress signal to me to come with her. I was taken to the same room as before, and as before the two men and the midget were there waiting for me. The only difference was that my violin was no longer there and *Shvester* was. She stood above the two men and smiled down at me. There was no sorrow or hurt in her eyes this time.

I looked at the man with the fat nose. He took a step forward.

"We will not waste time today. Your mother has already confessed. She has told us everything. Now you must confess. If your story is the same as hers, then neither of you will be hurt. What is your name?"

My mother has confessed? Had Bubbe made up some other story or were they just bluffing? I wondered. I had the feeling they were bluffing. Bubbe had told them nothing and they did away with her, as they would do with me, if I didn't tell.

"I told you, I know of no other name. I am Ewa Krisowski."

I don't know why I felt so calm. I stood before these two men and looked above them at *Shvester*. Perhaps I had accepted my fate.

I saw the hand rise up above my shoulder. As it came down upon me, I sank readily to the floor, no resistance to his hand.

The pain, which had been excruciating before and had made sleeping on my left side impossible, was minimal this time.

"Get up!" the man shouted.

I stood up.

"Where did you get those papers?"

"I have always had them."

This time he slapped my face, and again I moved in the direction of his hand so I felt only a slight sting down the left side of my face.

He asked me the same questions again and again, and I answered, and again and again he slapped me. At last, when he had drawn blood, he stopped.

"You will regret this," he said to me, and then turned to the wardress and said, "Cell D."

I was led away, back down the long corridor, all the way to the other end and up the same stairs we had come down when we had first arrived. Then we walked down another hallway. The wardress stopped in front of a door and held it open for me. It was the bathroom. There were no toilets in the cells, so every once in awhile I and the other prisoners were taken to the bathroom. I looked forward to this time more than anything else. It was a chance to get some water. I would go to the sink to wash my hands and face and allow the water to run into my mouth.

I didn't know whether the blood was coming from my nose or my lip, but the wardress allowed me time enough to splash the cold water over my face until the bleeding stopped.

I was then taken down yet another hallway and down three flights of stairs. I could feel the temperature change as we stepped down the last flight. The hallway was wet and cool, the walls made of stone. I could see drops of water oozing out of these stones as though they were being crushed by the weight of the building. The wardress unlocked the door and motioned me into a dark room. As I followed her in, I realized that *Shvester* was gone. Where was I going, I wondered, if she would leave me alone?

The wardress walked across to the other end of the room, unlocked another door, and motioned for me to go in. It was darker still. I could see shadows and movement; other people were already there. The door closed behind me and the key turned in the lock.

"Ewa?"

"Rachela?"

"Ewa! At last it is you!"

I stumbled forward, reaching out for my bubbe, and fell at last into her waiting arms. We sat on the floor rocking and holding on to one another, talking, laughing, and crying. Bubbe had told them nothing. They told her I was dead, but she knew it wasn't so. She had been in this dark cell since we had been separated, and had spent her hours between visits to the two men in prayer.

"What now, do you think?" I asked her when we had caught up with each other's lives.

"We will die," came a woman's voice from the other side of the cell. She spoke in Yiddish.

"Are we all Jews here then?" I asked.

"Who else would they put in a place like this? We will die tomorrow," the woman said.

I heard moaning and sobbing and praying. I held on to Bubbe, and we continued rocking.

We spent what appeared to be the next several days eating (yes, at last they were feeding us), sleeping, talking, going to the bathroom, and being questioned by the men upstairs.

Although I could never get a good look at her, I could tell that Bubbe was not standing up to the beatings very well. When she returned from the interrogations, she would hunch herself into one corner of the cell and ask to be left alone for a while. Eventually, she would come out of this retreat and reach out for me. When I huddled up close, I could feel her chest still heaving and smell the blood on her. Together we would pray for God to end our suffering.

One morning, a large wardress with her two front teeth missing opened the cell and bellowed in at us, *"Stehen Sie auf! Stehen Sie auf!* — Get up! Get up!"

For the first time since we had arrived, we were led outside into a courtyard. The air was cool and moist, but the sun was out and the day smelled sweet and clean; it was spring! We squinted at one another, trying to adjust to the bright sunlight. Each of us examined the others. We were a bloody, stinking crew. There were five of us; Bubbe was the oldest, I the young-est, and after me a petite Polish woman in her twenties and a set of French twins who claimed they were thirty-two but looked more like fifty-two.

Several guards were there to see that the five of us were loaded without mishap into the waiting prison van. The two tall men who had spent the last few weeks interrogating us came out into the courtyard.

"They want to wish us *bon voyage*, I am sure," said Dvora, the woman in her twenties.

As usual, the man with the fat nose did the talking. "En-tering the *Reich* with false documents is a serious crime, pun-ishable by death." With that said, he grinned and closed and locked the van door.

We could see nothing through the black-painted windows. We bounced along in silence until Lisette, one of the twins, began her usual whining about how she and her sister were really not Jewish.

"*C'est vrai!* — It's true! Only our grandmother was Jewish. Why should we be punished for that?"

"Why should any of us be punished for being Jewish?" I said.

Dvora agreed. "The world is crazy now."

Bubbe kept quiet. She knew to argue with the twins was futile and so did I, but it gave me something to do, something to think about besides death.

"We are French ballerinas. We have nothing to do with the Jews."

"You do now." Dvora laughed.

"The Polish are a stinking people. All Poles should be shot," said Liselle.

"You smell as bad as we do, and you look worse. And I think you two are dried-up old ladies. Ballerinas could never look so — so . . ."

"Chana, that is enough. It will do us no good to fight amongst ourselves. This may be our last hour alive and you are choosing to spend it this way."

Dvora leaned toward Bubbe. "What do you know?" she asked.

All of them had learned to trust Bubbe completely when it came to her premonitions. When she said we would be fed, we were fed. When she said the interrogators planned to trick us, there was a trick, but we were not trapped by it, and when she said nothing, we knew to watch out, one of us would get an extra beating that day.

"I cannot say for sure," she began, "but I believe we will be all right. It is best we each pray in silence, search out our own souls."

The twins sent up a loud wail.

"She is speaking of death. It is a nice way of saying we will die. I am not fooled," Lisette cried.

For the rest of the trip we listened to the sisters cry and moan at one another. Nothing Bubbe said could calm them down. When the van stopped, I was the first one at the door. Nothing could be worse than being trapped with the twins day after day.

The driver opened the doors and we climbed out and found ourselves outside another prison. New guards led us through the gates and into the building. Once again, they gave us showers and another set of prison clothes. Then they gave us each a piece of bread and a mug of watery cocoa.

To our delighted surprise, they gave us a cell with a skylight and allowed us to go outside once a day and parade in a circle around the courtyard for exercise.

A few days after we arrived, the interrogations began again. We learned to accept them as part of our daily routine, something to be endured if we were to continue to stay alive. All of us knew, without Bubbe telling us, that if we were to confess to anything, we would be shot.

After a week of daily exercises in the spring air, and regular mealtimes, the wardress—we called her *Der Hals*, the neck, because of her long neck and small head—assigned us each a job. Bubbe and I were both assigned kitchen duty.

"It will be all right now, Bubbe," I said one night as we were washing and drying the dishes. "It is better than the ghetto. It is not a lot of food—a bowl of soup and some bread and cheese—but we get it every day, and at night we have a comfortable place to sleep. If we cannot be out looking for Mama and Anya, then this is where I want to be. The war will be over soon, anyway."

CHAPTER SIXTEEN

Chana

FOR THE NEXT FEW MONTHS we worked hard in the kitchen, attended occasional interrogations, and took our daily exercise around the courtyard, watching spring turn into summer and then into fall. We were more able to keep track of the date, now that we could see day and night and the changing seasons. On what we guessed was July sixteenth, Bubbe surprised me with a birthday tomato she had somehow managed to get, or steal, from the kitchen. I didn't ask her about it. We split the ripe fruit in half and tried as best as we could to eat it slowly, savoring every juicy, meaty bite.

I was seventeen, the age Mama had been when she had Jakub, her first baby.

"And where am I, at seventeen?" I asked the fat bowl I was scrubbing one day. "I'm in prison, that's where. My life, my dreams, are nothing now. I have spent my years starving, wasting my mind, wasting my talents. I will never be a famous violinist. Think of all I have missed. Think of all I have yet to learn." I let my tears drop into the sink, plinking holes into the soapsuds. I cried some more so that I could watch my tears melt the suds. That was what I had become, someone who found entertainment in tears and suds.

One October morning the wardress did not come to roust

us out of our cell. By afternoon, when we had not been fed either breakfast or lunch, we all could sense that something bad was about to happen, and we looked to Bubbe to tell us what it was. Bubbe would only shake her head and remind us to be strong, to be with God. At last, in the evening, *Der Hals* came to the cell and unlocked the door. *"Stehen Sie auf! Schneller!*—Get up! Faster!" she shouted.

We shuffled through the door and trotted down the hallway after her. We were taken outside, where our interrogators were waiting for us. The night air was cold and blew through my uniform as if it wasn't even there.

"This is your last chance," said *Herr* Schacht, or *Trottel*, nincompoop, as we called him. "Any one of you who wishes to confess will be safe and will be allowed to remain here. Anyone so unwise as to ignore this offer will most assuredly die."

Yes, this man was stupid. Either way we died, we knew that. My teeth began to chatter.

A van rolled into the yard and two men got out.

Herr Trottel stepped up to the van. "Anybody?"

We remained silent.

"Your deaths will be most unpleasant. Shooting would be too easy for you. No, you will be sentenced to hard labor and, believe me, you will not last a week."

The two officers from the van came up behind us and shoved us into the back. Before we could disentangle ourselves, the van was speeding away, the cold air whistling through the doors like tiny sirens.

When we stopped, the officers let us out of the van, and we found ourselves at a train station teeming with people. Our driver told us to stand in the line on the left.

I looked at the long line of bedraggled people surrounded by armed guards. Where were we going? I saw the train, a black monster with black windows and black bars on those windows. Why, I wondered — and not for the first time — did the Nazis always make everything look evil? Why would they be so blatant about it? How could they be? I gazed across the tracks at the people who stood and watched our progression in the line. People who still had lives and families and food to eat. They were the reason Hitler could be so obvious. They were the reason this war against us, the Jews, could be so successful. They knew, they saw, and they did nothing but watch.

At the front of the line was a table with two SS — Defense Corps — officers sitting at it. When I got to them, one of the officers asked me my name.

"Ewa Krisowski," I said.

They didn't even blink. They searched through their stack of papers, pulled one out, and told me to sign it. I looked at the paper and saw my false name, my real name, my true birthdate, and my place of birth written at the top.

Then there were a lot of words I didn't have time to read. Two guards, one on either side, had closed in on me, waiting for me to sign. I bent over the paper and signed it, catching the line "Sentenced to hard labor for life" near the bottom.

"Please, God," I mumbled, "let this war end soon."

The inside of the train was dark and lined with small wire-mesh cells. Bubbe and I were stuffed into one of these small pockets with the twins, Dvora, and two other women. These two women kept staring at me and pushed their way between the others to get closer. They looked as if they wanted to eat me. I took Bubbe's hand in mine and moved toward her. More women were shoved into our cell, and I was stuck pressed up against Bubbe with the two vultures mashed up against my back.

We stood like this for hours, barely able to shift our bodies left or right. I had to go to the bathroom, but there seemed to be no toilets on this train. I felt something wet hit my legs. Had I lost control? I hadn't even felt it, and I still felt as if I had to go, badly.

"Bubbe, I think I just wet myself," I whispered.

"*Moi aussi* — Me, too," said the woman pressed into my back.

I shuddered.

A guard passed down the aisle and was besieged in several languages by women desperate to go to the bathroom.

"You will wait!" he shouted.

It was fine to say we would wait, but no one could, and puddles began to collect in all the cells. I was ashamed when at last I, too, could hold it no longer and felt myself letting go. I tried to push away from Bubbe, backing myself farther into the French woman behind me.

She spit at the back of my head.

"When will you learn, Chana?" Bubbe said.

I hung my head. When would I learn?

The train slowed down and came to a halt. Guards were suddenly everywhere.

"*Alles raus, schneller!*" they shouted.

They herded us out into the aisles and as we passed the guards, they took aim at us, beating us on the shoulders and head with their stubby batons.

"You have no self-control. You are animals!" they shouted at us.

As I approached a guard with a baton, I prepared myself

for the strike, pulling my arms in close to my body. I saw the guard draw his weapon up over his head, but before he had the chance to hit me, Bubbe slapped her hands on my back and pushed me forward, out of the way of the rod.

Bubbe received several blows to her head and shoulders for her trouble, blows that should have been mine.

They led us out of the train to a field, soft beneath our feet, under the stars, where they ordered us to squat down and do our business.

Would this night of shame never end?

We then climbed back onto the train, and they locked us back up in our cells.

The train lurched forward and we traveled for another five minutes before it stopped again. This time all the noise and commotion was on the outside. We could hear shouts and clomping boots and doors opening and shutting in other sections of the train. We remained there for hours, our hands and feet numb with our stillness. What were we waiting for? The noise outside had ended long ago, and still we waited.

Finally the train began to grumble and clank and we started to creep forward. A few minutes later we were on our way again.

I had shifted my position so I was now beside Bubbe and the two women were facing us, their cheesy breath suffocating me.

"Auschwitz," the taller woman said to us, her head bobbing on her neck.

We ignored her.

"We are going to Auschwitz," she said in German.

Bubbe nodded. "I know the place, Oświęcim, we call it. It is in Poland. Chana, we are returning to Poland."

"We die in Poland then," said the other woman.

"Why are we going to Oświęcim?" I asked Bubbe. "There is nothing there but swamp."

"To work, to starve, to die," said the shorter woman. "I have heard it is so. No one returns from this Auschwitz. Zola, over there"—she poked her finger through the mesh and pointed at a stiff, sticklike woman across the aisle—"she knows everything. She is a murderer."

I didn't know how to take this last piece of information. Did she know everything *because* she was a murderer? Had Zola really killed someone? Why was I believing these two women, one of whom had spit on my head?

"We are not all political prisoners then?" Bubbe asked.

"No. Many are thieves, murderers, true criminals. We are mishy-mashy, all mixed together."

We rode on, stopping again to go to a field, then filing back into the train, but never were we given food or water. We hadn't eaten since the night before.

Again we stopped, and the guards hurried down the aisle shouting, unlocking the cells, and yanking us out.

"We could not be stopping to go to the bathroom so soon, could we?" I asked Bubbe as we shuffled down the aisle.

"This must be Auschwitz," she replied.

We stumbled out of the train. Above us was a white station sign with black gothic lettering. I could only make out a few of the letters in the early dawn but, yes, this was indeed Auschwitz.

The guards charged forward, herding us into lines, beating us with their sticks, and using barking dogs to keep us moving.

All was noise and confusion as we scrambled along with hundreds of others as disoriented as we were.

The air was thick and sticky, the sky unnaturally pink. We could smell something cooking, burning. It must be some horrible animal, some fatty, rotten meat, I decided. I hurried forward with Bubbe, hoping that we'd soon pass through this thick, blanketing stench, but it was everywhere.

"Halt!" the guards shouted down the line as we approached a gate with letters strung across the top of it.

"*Arbeit Macht Frei*," Bubbe read. "Work Will Set You Free."

All around the gate was a high wall of electrified wire. We waited as people were pulled away from our lines and men were separated from the women and led through this gate. The rest of us were pushed on until at last we arrived at another gate, the entrance to a place they called Birkenau. Here the smell was even stronger, the pink sky almost red, the air closing in on us, feeding on us.

The guards marched us through this gate in rows of five and led us to the front of a long, low building, where two SS women in full uniform were waiting. They pushed us inside a room that smelled of disinfectant, reminding me of the time, now so long ago, when Estera Hurwitz and I were scrubbing the stairs for the Nazis. Whoever could have guessed then how great and cruel the imagination of a human full of hate could be?

"Remove your clothing and queue up for showers!" the SS women shouted.

I glanced over at the two men standing by the entrance. Bubbe stepped forward and spoke to one of the women.

"Please, she is modest, can she not . . . ?"

"How is it that you were not selected?" the officer asked

before Bubbe could finish her sentence. "You are too old. You will not live a day."

I studied Bubbe for the first time in a long while. Yes, it was true, she did look old, my youthful bubbe. She had lost so much weight that her skin hung on her bones like an empty burlap sack, and her hair, so black just three years ago, had gone gray like ashes—dull and dead.

"For what was I to be selected?" she asked them.

The two women smirked at one another.

"I am a nurse. Were they wanting someone to do a job? In prison I worked in the kitchen but I am fully qualified—"

"You were a prisoner?"

"Yes, political. We were sent here, sentenced to hard labor."

"Prisoner? Good. It was why you were not selected, but still you will not last. Now you will remove the rest of your clothes."

"But my—"

"Everyone!"

I thanked Bubbe for trying and removed my clothes, cowering behind her as we filed into a brightly lit shower room. The door closed behind us and the showers came on, a cold spray that felt better in my mouth than on my skin. We tried to drink as much as we could.

A door opened at the other end and a voice shouted, *"Heraus! Heraus!"*

Following orders, we hurried, dripping wet, out into another large, bare room where women in striped uniforms grabbed us by the hair and chopped it off. Another woman used a razor and ran it around the crown of our heads. Without time to think, I was shoved forward, where two women grabbed my arms and shaved my armpits. Another woman kicked my

legs apart and shaved between them. Again I was pushed forward, where I was doused with a shower of disinfectant that
stung like needles on my bare skin. Before I could figure out
what was happening, I was outside in the cold October air,
wet, naked, and shivering. I looked out in front of me and saw
the barbed wire everywhere, and beyond it, nothing, no trees
or grass or bushes. Like a warning it spoke to me — "Nothing
can grow here, nothing can live here."

CHAPTER SEVENTEEN

Chana

WHEN I TURNED AROUND, I found Bubbe standing behind me. We took a second to examine each other and then broke into hysterical laughter.

"You look like a baby bird, Bubbe."

"And you, Chana, you are Jakub without your hair."

"*Zugänge*, newcomers, here, quickly, quickly!" shouted another guard.

We filed into another building, where more women, prisoners also, handed out clothes. I was given a large dress that looked like a shirt, mismatched stockings, and two clogs — one too small and one too large for my feet. We began moving through the crowd, trading our goods for shoes and clothing that fit. In the end I found myself with clogs that were still too big but matched, and the same large dress; no one else wanted it except Bubbe, and I refused to let her trade it for her warm knickers and sweater. If she were to survive, I knew she would need to stay warm.

At the end of this long room were tables. At the first table they took down our names, our ages, and our professions. When the clerk in front of us saw Bubbe and heard that she was in her fifties she nodded and said, "Yes, you are thirty-eight."

"No, I think you misunderstood," Bubbe began.

"No one over forty should be here. Do you understand?"

Bubbe took the woman's hand. "Yes, thank you. You are very kind."

"I grew up in Lodz," said the clerk. "I moved away when I married. My name is Sora. We are sisters, no? I will look after you and try to get you a good job, but first you will have to survive quarantine. Most do not make it." She squirmed in her seat, glancing sideways at the other clerk. Then she turned to me. "And this is your daughter."

"No, I am her — I mean, yes, yes, I am her daughter."

"Yes, and I think twenty is a good age for you."

"Yes, I am twenty." I nodded.

"And what do you do? Your profession."

"Profession? I — nothing. I'm a student, or I was, once, long ago."

"She plays the violin," Bubbe said.

"Shh, Bubbe, what does that matter here?"

"It's wonderful!" The clerk beamed at me. "This could help you, they could always use another violinist."

"They? Who?"

The woman looked behind us and then leaned forward in her chair, her brown tufts of hair standing straight up on her head. She lowered her voice to a whisper. "I wonder, in your travels, if perhaps you have met Dovid and Ruchel Ozick, my mama and tata. You see, I have not heard." Her face, lined and waxy, harsh beneath her tufts of hair, suddenly softened. "I need to know if they are all right."

Bubbe leaned forward to speak, but the clerk held up her hand.

"Not now, the *Lagerführer* is coming to see why the line has stopped; you will have to move along."

Bubbe squeezed her hand. "I'm sorry, I can't tell you," she said, and then moved on to the next table.

At this table, two women tattooed numbers on the inside of our left forearms. They were quick and careless with the needle. Each jab into the skin made me jump. Even as I moved away from the table, I could feel the stinging, as though with every poke they had deposited a needle into a pore in my arm.

In our group all the digits in our numbers were the same except the last two or three. Bubbe's last number was 71 and mine 72. Everything here was orderly.

With the help of the SS guards and their dogs, we were organized into groups of five and marched along a hard-packed road to the quarantine block. Along the way we passed a low building with two tall brick chimneys rising up toward the sky, and from these came thick clouds of black smoke. I wanted to stop and watch the smoke. I wanted to stop and think a minute, but there was no time. *"Schneller! Schneller!"* they kept barking at us. "Faster!"

We were led through another set of barbed wire and before us stood row upon row of long, low stone huts. These buildings were grouped and divided by still more barbed wire and electrified fencing, and just in case that wasn't enough, they had tall watchtowers at the far corners of the compound where sentries kept an eye, and a rifle, poised on the movements of the inmates.

I took Bubbe's hand as we walked past the row of huts. Dead bodies were lying in piles in front of almost every barrack. They all looked alike — faceless, almost skinless piles of bones. How hard had these people fought for their lives? And now, if they could speak, would they say it was worth the fight? I wanted to know. I had to know. If that was to be my fate, to be tossed onto a pile and become a nameless, faceless nobody, why not die quickly and get it over with? Why should I allow myself to be tortured, why suffer, just to come to this? I looked down at the tattoo on my forearm. Who was I kidding? Already I had become nameless, and in this rag they had given me to wear and with my hair all shaved off, I was well on my way to becoming faceless.

I felt a hand ram me from behind. "Stay in your row!" boomed the voice now above me. The guard had pushed me to the ground. Somehow I had let go of Bubbe's hand and had fallen behind.

"Get up!"

I was already trying to get up when the guard slapped me down again. Again she shouted and again she slapped me down as I tried to get up.

What kind of game was this? I wondered, tears stinging my eyes. She wants me to get up but keeps slamming me down.

Before she could get at my aching shoulders again, I rolled away from her and in the same movement rolled up onto my feet. I ran along the line searching for Bubbe, but she was hard to find, everyone looked alike and no one looked human. They were marching creatures from some other world.

At last I saw a head turn, a glance, a pair of familiar eyes blinking at me. Bubbe! I ran up to her and fell in step. We couldn't speak to one another, but she grabbed my wrist and shook it. Pay attention, the shake said. Your life depends on it.

A whistle blew. "Halt!" commanded the guards all down the line. We stopped and then, like animals, like a herd of cows, we were shoved back behind the barracks. The dogs snapped at our legs, the guards slapped and swatted and kicked. Faster and faster they wanted us to move. What was the rush? Where was the fire? All morning they had hustled me along, spun me this way and that, with no explanation, no reason. It was enough. Who did they think I was? Who did they think they were?

I didn't know if it was the lack of food, or the lack of sleep, or just the confusion of the past few days, but it was as if my mind just exploded. I couldn't take it anymore. They had killed Tata and expected me to feel nothing, to accept it, to go on. They had worked and starved Zayde to death, and again I was supposed to take it. I was an animal, without feelings, a Jew. Then Anya and Mama, my whole family torn from me in every ugly, evil way Hitler's army could devise, and I was supposed to accept it all. Who could endure such a thing? Who? Who?

I turned back toward the guard, the one with the gun. Yes, it was time to see how they liked it. Time for them to see how it feels to watch someone you care about get her face blown off. It would be easy to grab the weapon away from her. Easy to pull the trigger and watch her face explode. It didn't matter that it would be the last thing I did. It didn't matter that I was about to commit the worst possible crime, the worst sin. God was already punishing me; now at least I would have given Him a reason. That was what was destroying me the most. There was no reason. Nothing made sense. The whole world had gone crazy. The good were punished, the evil rewarded. Now it was my turn to hand out the punishment.

I fought my way through the crowd of women being shoved forward. The more I fought, the angrier I got, so by the time I had reached the guard, my whole body was heaving.

The guard was so busy pushing the women forward and shouting her commands that she didn't see me approaching. Yes, I could grab the gun easily. I took another step forward. She looked up and saw me. I froze and it seemed as if everything around me came to a standstill. Only my mind kept moving, kept seeing. I was seeing myself breathing hard chunks of air, in and out, in and out. I saw myself in my baggy shirtdress that hung down to my ankles, and in my clogs, hard, the bottoms worn on one side. I could see my bald head, my skin stretched over my nose and my cheeks, and I knew that this was all I was. I was not a girl with dreams of someday becoming a great violinist, or of getting married and having children. I was not a girl with a family, or a house, or fancy clothes. I was not someone who belonged to a *shul*, or who was known for her brown wavy hair with a strand that always jutted out in the back. I could no longer identify myself by what I owned, or who I knew, or what my dreams were. This—my body, my mind, my soul—was all I was. It is all any of us ever are, and without the camouflage of my dreams and possessions, I realized that everything I did, every thought I had, was all I was. Here in this place, in this skin, my actions and thoughts would be magnified. It was all very simple. If I killed the guard, all of who I was would be a murderer, not a murderer and a violinist who lived in a house and had a nice family—just a murderer. If I showed love, all of me would be a lover. Who then did I want to be?

Facing the guard, I opened my mouth to speak and her gun came crashing down on my head.

The next thing I knew I was looking up into the faces of many strangers, all looking alike and yet none of them familiar.

"She's awake."

I twisted around and saw that I was lying with my head in Bubbe's lap. Her knickers were stained with blood.

"Chana, this place we're in, this Auschwitz, we must be careful. You cannot just—"

"I know, Bubbe. I understand now. It won't happen again."
I tried to sit up, but my head was too heavy.

A woman I had never seen before crouched down beside
me and took my hand. The other faces moved away. "To survive
here you must be smarter than they are. We cannot act as they
do; they will always win. They have the weapons and the dogs
and the world on their side. We have only ourselves."

"And God, praised be He," Bubbe added.

"God? God? No. God is not on our side. God is nowhere!"
I tried to sit up again. This time I succeeded. I looked around
and saw that I was in a clay courtyard behind the barracks.
There were no trees, grass, or flowers, just groups of women
clustered about doing nothing but shivering and talking or
sleeping on the hard clay.

"Chana, do you really feel that is so?" Bubbe asked. "Do
you really think God is nowhere?"

"I don't know. I'm tired of trying to find God. Why doesn't
He find me? Why doesn't He save me? You believe everything
without questioning. But I have so many questions. There is
so much I don't understand."

"Hardship and suffering should not lessen our love for God.
Everything we do, even here, should remain as it has always
been, a means of communion with God. Remember, there is
nothing, nothing here on this earth that is apart from the *Shek-
hinah*, God's presence."

I wanted to scream. My head was spinning and Bubbe was
trying to make sense out of nonsense.

"How can you say that?" I said to her. "Look at the Nazis.
Look at what they are doing to us. Didn't you see those bodies
piled up in front of the buildings?"

Bubbe nodded. "The guards, the SS, have done that, not
God. Do not confuse the things people do to one another with

what God does and is. It is their sins that make God seem so far away, but if we call upon Him in truth, He is here."

"Well, have you not called upon Him in truth? Why then are we here? Why would God let us come to this? I am so hungry my own arm is starting to look good. No, God is nowhere."

The woman who had been listening to us argue, spoke up. "Do not fill your head with such things. I have been here already four weeks and I have learned that to think is to die."

"That makes no sense," I said. "You said we must be smarter than they are and now you say not to think at all. Who are you?"

The woman held out her hand. "My name is Rivke. I am from Poland, also, from Czernica, in the east. You will see for yourself soon enough that what I say is true."

"What is this place?" I indicated the area around us. "What are we doing here?"

Rivke laughed. Her laugh was pretty, musical, and all her movements and gestures were graceful. I wondered for an instant if I could make myself move the way she did, but with my head still hurting I was happy just to be sitting up.

"We are in what the *Blockälteste*, block senior, calls the 'meadow.' It is pretty, no?" She sang another note of laughter. "We stay here all day. We cannot go inside. Inside it is worse, but there is cover when it rains. I would like to be there when it rains, no matter the smell."

"But it cannot be any worse than this smell out here. I think maybe someone has stuffed my nose with *trayf*, unkosher meat."

Rivke sucked in her breath. "You are not far from the truth. They pretend here, and we, too, pretend. We are not supposed to know, or to talk about it."

"To know what? To talk about what?"

"Enough, Chana," Bubbe said. "You ask too many questions. You should try to lie back down. Your head, it still bleeds a little."

I felt the back of my head. It was sticky. I was sorry about Bubbe's knickers, but I did not want to change the subject.

"No, I want to know," I said. "I am not a little girl, Bubbe." I looked at the glances exchanged between Bubbe and Rivke and then, somehow, I knew. I knew, and I realized I had known all along, but my mind had refused to understand. The smells, the smoke in the chimneys — it was human flesh, human hair and bones burning. I was drenched in it, choking with it, but I knew that in order for me to live, I had to breathe, I had to inhale this residue of someone else's life.

It seemed that we had been in the camp, in the meadow, for days before we were given our first meal, but Bubbe assured me it had only been hours since they had first shoved us back behind the barracks. Two young women with swollen legs and bare feet carted the meal in a large drum on two wheels to the center of the yard.

Rivke stood up. "I must go now. I can talk with you later. You will not get your own bowl today; that you will have to organize. Oh, and stay to the back of the line when they serve, because all the real bits of food are at the bottom of the drum." Rivke started to walk away and then turned back around and added, "Also, drink your soup, no matter what. Chana, do not think about it, just drink it."

I watched her walk away from us, and then Bubbe helped me stand up. My head was throbbing. "Is it all right back there?" I asked Bubbe. "It stings."

"A good gash you have there, but Rivke said it is dangerous to go to the hospital. People rarely return."

I followed Bubbe into the line behind Dvora and Lisette

and Liselle. "Do you trust this Rivke?" I asked Bubbe. "She says the strangest things, I think. Maybe she has been here too long and her mind is gone."

"She has been here four weeks, a week more than the average, so she has learned some things about surviving here. Yes, I trust her, and I think we need her. Maybe she needs us as well."

We had to share our bowl of soup with Dvora and the twins. Every newcomer had to share a bowl with four others. The soup looked like weak tea with disgusting bits of food floating on top. It smelled like old socks and tasted worse.

"You can have my share," I said to the others. "I do not feel well enough to even look at this."

Bubbe stamped her foot. "Chana, enough of this! Rivke said do not think, just drink. Now, here, you close your eyes, you hold your nose, but you drink."

"It is poison, but I will drink it, Bubbe. And then I will be sick."

After our soup we were left again to stand, sit, or lie on the clay. The wind had begun to blow harder and the clouds to darken. Dvora, Bubbe, and I huddled together trying to keep warm, and the twins, who had found fellow French-women, left to form their own huddle.

Rivke returned from her own block and wrapped her arms around us. "We will be a family together, we four," she said. "I can help you organize some things: spoons, bowls, a sweater for Chana, some smaller shoes for Dvora."

"Organize?" Dvora said. "I don't understand."

"Yes, here we 'organize' things—trade, bargain, steal, whatever it takes to get what you need to stay alive."

"I will get by all right with my big shoes." Dvora shuddered. "I do not need to steal things. Stealing is wrong."

I nodded my agreement. Bubbe remained silent and still.

Rivke lowered her head. "I will not feel guilty for what I have done here. I trade and bargain where I can, but yes, I steal, too — not from the living, but from the dead."

"That is even worse!" I said.

"No, you will see. What does a dead person need with a piece of bread or a warm coat? It keeps me alive. I need that bread. I need what they leave behind. Don't make me feel guilty for trying to live. I have hurt no one, and you will see many Jews — prisoners like us — help the Germans. They agree to whip us and beat us so they can have a better place to sleep, or more food, or a kerchief for their head. I have hurt no one."

Rivke was in tears by now. Dvora and Bubbe wrapped their arms around her and hugged her. I sat down on the ground. My head hurt. I felt overwhelmed by what this woman with the pretty hands and graceful movements was saying. I wanted to think. I just wanted everything to stop happening and people to stop talking so I could think about things.

Rivke crouched down beside me. "You will not forgive me?"

I looked away.

"Today, this morning, I lost my sister. She is dead with typhus, and my friend Genia, she was taken yesterday for *Aus-senarbeit*, outside work. She is in another block now. I need you as my family, and I can help you. It is a fair exchange, but not if you do not want me."

"I am sorry about your sister. I have lost, too. I am just so confused. I think it is this crack on the head."

Rivke leaned forward and kissed my forehead. "You can lie on my lap."

I got up onto my knees and hugged her. She, along with Bubbe and Dvora, was my family now.

Whistles began blowing on the other side of the block and

before I knew what was happening, Rivke had grabbed me and had started running. Dvora and Bubbe followed behind, along with many other women. We hid ourselves between two huts. We could hear a woman thrashing a whip and barking out orders. "Sixteen girls for *Aussenarbeit*. You there, and you." The whip cracked and the women screamed and moaned until sixteen women had been rounded up. When all was silent, we came out from our hiding spot.

"They will work you to death if you get caught in one of those roundups. We are better off here for now," Rivke explained to us.

The day dragged on. It started to rain, gently at first, and then in sheets. I was freezing, but even more than that, I was thirsty. I opened my mouth and let the water run in. I laughed out loud as I imagined the guards all running around trying to keep it from raining so we couldn't drink. Bubbe used the rain to get the blood on my head and her knickers cleaned off, thanking God for such a gift. The water was wonderful, but when I had had enough to drink and my head was clean, I wanted it to stop. By late afternoon the ground had turned into a gray mush that sucked at our clogs as we paraded around in circles. I began to hum to myself, keeping time with our pacing, and then Bubbe joined in, and then Dvora and Rivke. We were all humming when I heard the music. I heard violins and a flute and cymbals and a drum, playing real music — or was it? Had the hit on my head caused me to start hearing things? I stopped pacing. "Do you hear that?" I asked. "Do you hear the music?"

"That's for the work parties. They are returning," Rivke explained.

"Real music? Here? How bad can it be if we are to be entertained by real music. It is wonderful!" I ran to the side of the hut and peered out. The band was playing a Sousa march, and marching through the mud to the music were thousands of women in rows of five. All of them were filthy. Their clothes were torn and their bare feet bloody and swollen. Their arms and legs, faces and heads were covered with sores and gaping wounds. Most of them tried to step lively as they passed under the eyes of the SS guards, but some didn't seem to care, didn't even seem to know where they were. Their heads were bobbing on their necks with every step they took, their shoulders drooping, their eyes vacant. Others were virtually being carried in, supported on either side by a helpful shoulder. They were all dying. For many, keeping in step with the music looked as if it would be the last thing they would do on this earth. The thought made me sick. Why did the orchestra keep playing? Why didn't they slow it down so the workers could keep up? They were prisoners, too — couldn't they see they were killing these people with their music? Never, in all of my wild imaginings, could I have come up with something as horrible as this. Now even music had become something ugly, something evil. I felt as if the Nazis had somehow discovered everything I ever cared about and then had set about destroying it all one by one. There was nothing left. Nothing!

"See those women? See them dragging in?"

I jumped. I didn't know Rivke had come up behind me. She was pointing to the women with the floppy heads and vacant stares.

I nodded.

"That is what happens to people who think too much. They become what the people here call *Muselmänner*."

"*Muselmänner?* That means Muslims. I don't understand."

"It is the name given to those who have given up all hope. They have lost it here." Rivke pointed to her head. "There is nothing up there anymore and the body, it follows the mind.

They will be dead today, tomorrow at the latest. Remember that, Chana. You think too much. It is dangerous. The body can endure a lot if the mind will allow it. You must want to live more than anything else because here that is all there is — life, or death. But mostly death."

CHAPTER EIGHTEEN

Hilary

"I THOUGHT I SAW A GHOST for a minute. Baby, I thought I saw you going into the bathroom down on the fifth floor. This girl, she had long blond hair like yours before you cut it and a jacket like the one Brad gave you for your birthday with 'Aryan Warriors' written on the arm. You know? Hilary?

"You're looking funny. You look — you don't look good. No, your heart monitor, I don't think it should be doing that. You're — you're dying — someone — I've got to get someone. . . .

"What's that? Hey, what's — "

"Ah, Mrs. Burke, glad I spotted you in there. It's the fire alarm. You'll have to take the exit at the end of the hall. Just follow the others, please. Your daughter will be fine."

"What? Are you crazy? My baby, she's dying. Nurse, listen to me! Please come in here, she's dying! Get a doctor! Any doctor."

"Please try and stay calm. We'll take care of your daughter. If there's anything wrong, one of the nurses will see it on the monitor, but I have to ask you to get out of the building."

"Didn't you hear me? Come here. Look at this monitor! She's dying! I know she is."

"My God! Yes, okay, I'll get someone right away, but you must get out of the building."

"Hurry — my baby. Dear God, my baby.

"Hilary, I'm here. I'm staying right here. I won't leave, I promise. Don't you worry. Come on, fight!

"Where are they? Please, dear God, where are they? You're slipping away and the doctors are all out on the lawn directing traffic.

"God! Help me!"

Shema Yisrael, Adonai Elohainu Adonai Ehad.

CHAPTER NINETEEN

Chana

WE HAD BEEN in the Auschwitz-Birkenau concentration camp for only three weeks, and yet the changes I had seen in the people around me, in myself, were changes that would normally require the passage of several years. A woman could march out of camp with her head held high, her back strong and straight, and a glint in her eye, and return from work that afternoon a destroyed, broken mass of flesh, too far gone to make it much past the gate. Every day here was a lifetime, and with the passage of each day, I wondered if it was worth the struggle. I had no answer, and much to Bubbe's frustration, I was fast becoming one of the ragged people, the *Muselmänner*, I had seen dragging into camp toward the end of our first day.

I knew if it weren't for Bubbe I wouldn't have lasted this long, but I didn't feel gratitude. Sometimes I didn't think I felt anything, except rage — rage at everything and everyone, including Bubbe. She seemed to live on nothing but her beliefs, and I seemed to be dying by mine, yet I couldn't change. I didn't know how.

Every morning the kitchen workers handed out to each of us a chunk of black bread smeared with rancid margarine, which was to last us the day. I always ate mine at once and counted on Bubbe to give me some of hers later when I needed it, as I had done with Anya in the ghetto. I also counted on her to give me some of her soup in the afternoon and to sleep next to me and keep me warm at night. But others, too, had learned to count on her. She told them stories in the courtyard, stories she used to tell me. She wrapped their sore, freezing feet in bits of rags she had organized, and gave them her food. She held them in her arms and cried with them. She had become everyone's grandmother, and even women older than she were calling her Bubbe.

One day as groups huddled together behind the barracks, Bubbe saw me go off on my own, as I had done the past two days, and came after me.

"Chana, this has gone on long enough!"

I turned away. "Go to your friends, Bubbe. They need you."

"So, you think you will punish me. It is you whom you are hurting. You are going to allow yourself to waste away, to punish me?"

"You give them your food, you wash their faces and their sores with your tea."

"You want me to help only you?" she asked as she eased herself onto the ground.

"Yes, I mean no, it's just — don't you care that I'm — I'm dying? Bubbe, it's too much, what's the point of it all?"

Bubbe took my hand in hers. "Chana, what I give these people, what I try to give you, isn't enough, can never be enough. So many of them die. No matter what I do, they still die. I cannot give them, or you, the will to live, and without that, there is not even a hope of surviving here."

"There is not even a hope anyway," I said.

"If you feel that way, Chana, then you will die, and I will die with you."

I looked into her face. I held out my arms. "Bubbe, help me."

She grabbed my arms and pulled me into her lap as though I were a little girl. She rocked me in her arms and whispered, "Chana, please, do not think so much. Just do as they say."

Do not think. Always, do not think. But how could I stop? The Germans had taken everything, and now I was expected to give them my mind as well.

That next morning I felt too sick to get up for *Zählappell*, roll call. It was four in the morning; our *Blockälteste* had already blown her whistle and shouted into our hut for us to get up. Our hut was lined with bunks made out of slats of wood, three tiers high and separated by brick walls. We slept on a thin smattering of straw that reeked of the blood, pus, and urine it had absorbed as our rotting bodies slept, five to a bunk. Again I was not to think about it, I was just supposed to climb in and go to sleep. I was supposed to ignore the fat bugs that fell between the slats above me and onto my neck every time someone in the bunk above tried to turn over.

"Don't think, sleep," I would tell myself over and over as I waited for that blessed sleep. "Don't think, eat," as I swallowed my soup. "Don't think, march; don't think, pee; don't think, stand, starve, freeze, bleed, rot!"

Bubbe pulled herself out of the bunk with the others and then waited for me to follow.

"No, Bubbe," I said. "This is it. I am going to be one of the dead bodies they drag outside and drop at the end of the rows for *Zählappell*."

Bubbe felt my head. "You are warm. What else?"

"My stomach. I'm afraid if I move it will explode. All night I had to keep climbing out of bed and using the bucket."

Bubbe looked down at the end of the hut where the overflowing bucket stood. They fed us so little and yet we all seemed to be in constant need of a bathroom.

"Hurry then. You must get to the pits before *Zählappell* —
who knows how long it will last today."

We had roll call twice a day, and since we had been there
it had lasted anywhere from two to eight hours, but Rivke had
said it could last as long as twenty-four if the numbers didn't
add up correctly.

I did as Bubbe said and shuffled along to the lavatory hut.
Hundreds of women sat on the holes on either side of me. These
holes were cut out of thick slabs of concrete supported above
dug-out pits by another long concrete pedestal. There were
three of these conveniences in this building, and each ran almost
the full length of the hut and had approximately eighty to a
hundred holes. Still, we usually had to sit two to a hole, using
this time before *Zählappell* to get information, organize some
items, or just chat. This morning, no one wanted to sit with
me. They could tell I was sick and most believed that to even
look my way was to catch whatever I had. Once on my hole,
I couldn't get off and Bubbe and Dvora had to pull me off and
drag me back to our hut in time for *Zählappell*. No one missed
roll call, not even the dead.

As usual we were whipped into rows of five, facing forward,
standing straight and still. Bubbe and Dvora hustled me to the
back row and stood me up between them. My feet did not want
to support me. I knew I was going to be sick again and I could
only hope that being in the back row would keep me hidden
enough so I wouldn't get caught. Every time the *Blockälteste*
had passed us, Bubbe and Dvora would lean me against the
wall behind us, and I would sag to my knees and wait until it
was time to hoist myself up again.

"It's Taube!" Dvora whispered. She and Bubbe pulled me
to my feet. I tried to look up, to look alive, to forget that my

insides were running down my legs, as the *Rapportführer*, roll-call leader, strutted in front of us.

Taube was the man upon whom I had placed all my fears and hatred. I had seen this man extinguish a life in less than a minute simply by butting the person to the ground with his rifle and stomping on her neck.

While those around me tried to keep their teeth from chattering, I stood there trying not to sweat. The more I fretted about this, the more I sweated, so by the time Taube had reached our group, the top half of my shirtdress was soaked. Bubbe and Dvora closed in on me, squeezing me between them.

"What is that smell?" Taube demanded.

Was he speaking about me? Could he smell me from all the way up front? No, it couldn't be. How could he distinguish my diarrhea from all the other wretched odors in this camp? I locked my knees and held up my head. I was sweating more now and needed to spit, needed to . . . I dropped to my knees and threw up. I was gagging, choking. Nothing came out but clear slimy liquid, but the noise and my movements brought Taube to the back row.

"*Raus! Raus!*" he commanded.

Was he going to make me stand up only to butt me with his rifle and stomp on my throat?

I forced myself to stand. I had to show him I was strong, that this problem was only temporary.

"You are disgusting!" he said as I looked up at his face. "You think it is all right to make a mess like this? You like standing in your own mess? For this you will have *Sport*, all of you." He waved his hand above him, including the whole block in his gesture. "For as long as this *Appell* lasts you will stay down on your knees, all of you. Now! And you"—he pointed a gloved finger at me—"you will kneel right where you are standing."

I fell to my knees with the others.

Taube called to our *Blockälteste*'s assistant, Gerte, a short, dark Jew with brown teeth. "You see to it that she keeps her arms out as high as her shoulders. If they drop, use your whip." He spun around on his heel and marched away, leaving me to face Gerte. I knew it would do me no good to try to plead with this woman. To her, I was Jewish scum and she was Jewish royalty. Rumor had it that she had tossed her own mother and sisters onto the truck that took them to their death. Now she kicked Bubbe and Dvora aside with her warm-booted foot and circled around me, daring me with her sausage breath, heavy on my head, to just try to move.

I could see Bubbe out of the corner of my eyes murmuring her prayers for me. I wanted to shout at her and tell her to stop. She was wasting her time. God wasn't going to save me, or her, or anyone. I remembered how just yesterday evening, Bubbe had been whipped for stepping on the *Blockälteste*'s foot when Bubbe was leaving the hut. I remember how she just stood there and took it, her expression serene, as though she were walking through a field of poppies. And when the whipping was over, Bubbe looked at the woman with such pity, as if she had been the one who was whipped.

Never, *never* could I look at Gerte that way. Never could I "find God," as Bubbe claimed to do when confronted with something unbearable.

I decided my bubbe wasn't real. She was like my *shvester*, someone only of the imagination. She continued to murmur beside me, but Gerte left her alone. For some reason Gerte was afraid of my gentle bubbe. Perhaps she, too, sensed that Bubbe was not real, or maybe she was saving her beatings just for me.

My arms were numb from the shoulders out and my knees were sinking deeper into the mud and slime. I was shaking from head to foot, but something in me refused to allow my arms to slip below my shoulders.

I saw someone in front of me fall forward on her face. If she didn't move, she'd suffocate in the mud. Bubbe kept praying and the woman in front of me did not move. I was determined to make it, to remain on my knees, my arms raised as long as it took, if only to shut Bubbe up and to lift that woman out of the mud. If she died, it would be my fault.

At last the whistles blew and *Zählappell* was over. Dvora and Bubbe got up off their knees and rushed forward to congratulate me. I ignored them and crawled forward on my hands and knees to where the woman had fallen in the mud. She hadn't moved since she had fallen. I grabbed her shirt and rolled her over onto her back. Her face was plastered in mud, her mouth full of it, her eyes open and muddy. I dug the mud out of her mouth and shook her.

Gerte kicked me in the side. "She's dead, you idiot. You killed her, and that one over there." She pointed to another woman farther away. "You are like me now. How does it feel?"

Before I could speak, Bubbe had rushed forward with Dvora and grabbed me under the arms. Together they pulled me backward, toward the hut.

"Not so fast," came the *Blockälteste*'s voice from behind. Her name was Holga and she looked, to my mind, like what every German bully should look like. She was a large, almost fat woman with tiny, deep-set blue eyes and hair down to her shoulders, mocking our baldness. She wore no makeup except lipstick. Always she wore lipstick. We believed she even slept with it, freshly applied each night before going to bed.

"You." Holga pointed at me. "You are on *Scheisskommando*. Get along now."

I looked up at Bubbe. I felt too weak to move. I had hoped I could somehow hide myself away in one of the bunks before they locked the hut, and sleep there all day.

"Be strong, Chana," Bubbe whispered. "You made it through *Sport*. You are not a *Muselmann* yet."

"Enough of this! Go!" Holga kicked at me.

At the entrance to the lavatory hut the *Kapo*, work party leader, handed me an empty bucket and a small shovel. She gave me no instructions, but I really didn't need any. The work was easy enough. I was to scoop out the mess beneath each hole, dump it in the bucket, and haul it away to yet another pit. There were three others working in my row. They had already begun down near the entrance, so I took the center and dug the shovel into the first hole. As I scooped out the mess and dumped it, I thought about the fecal workers in the ghetto. I remembered how we used to pretend they weren't even there when they came along our street to clean up our messes. We knew the people with that job never lasted long because of typhus and other diseases that were easy to pick up, and I wondered if it was the same here. Was this the worst job? Did I already have typhus? Was that why I felt so sick? I didn't care. Just keep moving, I told myself. Move until you can no longer move. Move until you die. Then they won't have the pleasure of kicking the life out of you.

One of the workers on the opposite side came up to the hole in front of me and began digging.

"I'm Matel," she whispered, keeping her face down so the guard at the entrance wouldn't see her talking.

I said nothing. I kept digging. What did I care if she was Matel? I didn't want to make any more friends. I didn't want to care about anyone else. I said nothing to her, but every once in a while I couldn't help glancing up at her and trying to get a better look. She was slightly taller than I was, but for some reason I had the feeling she was young, very young.

During our lunch break, when they gave us the same meager helping of old sock soup, Matel came up to where I was sitting and sat down.

"I am sick," I said, not even bothering to look up. "You might catch it, go away."

Matel put down her bowl and scooted closer to me. She fingered the edge of my dress, and then saw me watching and pulled her hand away.

I looked into her eyes. She was very young.

"Sorry," she said. "You look like my mother. You are not as tall, or as old, but your face, it is — is gone like hers."

"Gone?"

"*Muselmann*. You know the expression?"

I looked away. I could see the guard moving toward us. Our lunch break was almost over.

"If I had been able to stay with Mama she never would have died, but they told her I was dead. They put her to work carrying heavy rocks and one day I saw her, looking even worse than you, dragging herself toward the camp after work. I called out to her, but she did not hear. She looked right at me, but she did not see. Do you understand? I was not real to her. She had dreamed of finding me so many times that when she really saw me, she could not believe I was not just another one of her dreams. That must be what happened. Do you not agree?"

I didn't answer. "Do you want my soup?" I asked her. "The break will be over in a minute. I cannot drink this today. You have it."

Matel paused only a second before grabbing my bowl and

pouring the soup into her dish. She drank it down, wiped her mouth with her sleeve, and smiled.

The whistle blew. It was time to get back to work.

When I returned to the hut that afternoon, Bubbe was not there. I searched for Dvora and found her in the crowd making their way to the lavatory.

"Dvora, please, what has happened? Where is Bubbe?" I asked when I caught up with her.

"A woman named Sora came and got her. You remember, the clerk? The one from Lodz, who said she would help us?"

"Yes, yes, but where is she? Where have they taken her?"

"It is good, Chana, she has inside work. She is a nurse at the *Revier*, camp hospital. It is where she needs to be."

"But I need to talk to her. I need to see her. I need to tell her that I am feeling a little better. It must not be typhus."

"She will try to see you. She said for me to tell you that." Dvora paused just outside the lavatory. "You do look better. Your face — your eyes look better, I think."

"I met a girl. A real girl, only twelve years old. She wants . . . It is silly, but she wants me to be her family, her mother. She wants me."

I left Dvora at the lavatory entrance and walked back toward my hut, wishing that I could have something to eat. I did not look forward to standing through another *Zählappell* today without food in my stomach, and for a moment I wished I hadn't given my soup away, but then, on second thought, remembering Matel, I was glad I had.

In front of me, I saw one of the non-Jewish prisoners walking with a package under her arm. Non-Jews were able to receive care packages from home. There was something odd about this package, though. It almost looked as if something were leaking out one of the ends. I ran forward and crept up behind the woman. Sure enough, white granules were pouring out of the bottom corner of the package. I stuck my bowl out in front of me and trotted along behind her, collecting the little granules in my bowl. When the woman with the package turned around I quickly headed in the opposite direction, my bowl gripped between my hands.

When I had a chance, I stopped, licked my finger, and dipped it into my bowl. I then poked my finger into my mouth and tasted the sweetest, most delicious taste in all the world — sugar!

CHAPTER TWENTY

Chana

BY THE END OF THE SIXTH WEEK, very few of the group of women from our train were left. Those of us who were, were taken to the sauna, or shower hut, and given cold showers, our first since we had arrived. We had learned to be wary of showers since we discovered that the Germans used the pretense of showers for gassing thousands of the prisoners who arrived by train each day. We were never sure what they had in store for us at any moment. They counted on our confusion and fear to keep us off balance, which was easy to do in our deteriorating condition. We never knew when the end was at hand.

This time, though, we really had showers and then got mopped with disinfectant and handed clean, although worn, clothes. I grabbed some knickers and a heavy shirt and threw them on before anyone could yank them out of my hands. In the past few weeks I had begun to see myself in a different light. I was an animal. I gave myself the eyes and mind of an animal, watching, waiting, listening. At last I understood what Rivke and Bubbe meant when they said, "Don't think." With animals, survival is by instinct, and by instinct I, too, would survive. I no longer tried to reason. I no longer held out any expectations. If at any moment I was alive, that was all that mattered. It was enough to eat, sleep, stay warm, and visit the lavatory hut twice a day. For that, I lived.

I was no longer on *Scheisskommando* but was put to work digging trenches, along with Dvora, Matel, and Rivke, whom I had not seen since she had left quarantine four weeks earlier. The twins were not in our block. They had been given a "special assignment."

It happened one afternoon, a week before the end of quarantine. Whistles blew throughout the camp and we heard the dreaded shouts of *"Lagersperre! Lagersperre!"* Everyone was confined to her block until "selection" was over. When the *Blockälteste* entered our hut with a clipboard in her hands, we knew that our group was to face selection. From the single window at the front of our hut I could see four men marching down the *Lagerstrasse*, main road. One of them was an armed guard who stepped inside and ordered us to remove our clothes and line up outside. *"Schneller!"* he shouted, before ducking back out and entering the next hut. Always it was *"Schneller!"*

Naked, I stepped outside into the icy damp behind Dvora, clutching my arms over my breasts. I saw *Rapportführer* Taube standing beside the guard and prayed he wouldn't recognize me.

"Stellen Sie an!—Line up!" he ordered.

My kneecaps began to jiggle up and down with a mind of their own as we shuffled into our rows of five.

Standing a few feet away from Taube were two other men: *Lagerführer* Hössler, in charge of camp discipline, and a man I had never seen before. This stranger was in full uniform, right down to his white gloves, and he stood before us like a fairy-tale prince, majestic and handsome. He stepped forward and ordered the first row to parade before him, left arms out so their numbers could be checked off as they passed.

They were a sorry sight, trying hard not to shuffle or stumble or slouch as they passed before this man. Their hair and bodies were caked in dirt and blood, infested with lice, and coated with a frozen layer of sweat. I glanced down at my own body. I was no better.

Row after row paraded before this man, and as each woman stood directly in front of him, he would run his eyes over her body and point either to the left or the right. I saw Jutka, an older woman like Bubbe, shuffle forward. She had been miserable without her husband, who was in the men's camp, and tried to get on any work party that was going out, in the hopes of seeing him pass by. The work had taken its toll on her. Her back was bent forward in spasms that only rest could mend, but she was not allowed to rest. As she stood before the man, she pulled herself up, her whole body trembling. He hardly glanced her way. He pointed to the left.

Most of the women were being sent to the left, so I was determined to go to that side as well. When Lisette stepped before him, our *Blockälteste* stepped forward with her clipboard and whispered something in the stranger's ear. His face lit up and he took Lisette by the hand and pulled her to his side. Liselle was next and again he pulled her away from the group and stood her on his other side. They looked like bookends, and the stranger looked delighted.

When our row was called forward, I took a deep breath, stood up as tall as I could, and stepped forward with every ounce of confidence I could muster. This handsome man would see I was worth keeping around. As I approached him, however, I saw both Dvora and Matel get sent to the right. I didn't know what to do. They looked as fit as anyone. They looked better than the twins, far better than Jutka. I looked at both lines again, the one on the left, then the one on the right. Everyone on the right, all twenty of them, appeared far healthier than most of the women on the left. But it was impossible! There were at least three hundred women standing to the left. Three hundred women who had spent the past six weeks struggling to stay alive, fighting starvation, going forward, picking themselves up again and again no matter how many times they had been beaten. They couldn't all be "going up the chimney," as our *Blockälteste* liked to say when she was sure no official could hear. Perhaps this was not a selection for death but for some different kind of work. I no longer knew which side to choose — as if I would be given a choice.

It was my turn to stand in front of the stranger. I looked down at my feet as I felt his gaze upon me and then, holding my hands in tight fists, I looked up, all the way up, into his eyes. There was nothing there. I couldn't even say what color they were. They were like smoky diamonds, facetless and cold. I was reminded of the stories Zayde used to tell me when I was six years old and already learning that I was quite good at the violin. He would hold me in his lap and rock me in the hush of his bedroom, where he liked to sit, and he would whisper in my ear, warning me about the evil eye and how its dark forces sought to possess any beautiful or especially talented child. I used to imagine that singular eyeball staring down at me while I slept, staring at me the way this stranger did now. I could not give in to the evil eye. I held my head even higher and put my hands on my hips. I would stare him down.

The stranger opened his mouth to say something, stopped, chuckled, and pointed to the right.

When the selection was over, more than four hundred women had been chosen for gassing. I didn't watch them leave, I didn't look over toward the tall chimneys that coughed up smoke day and night. If I looked, if I accepted this as real, I knew it would happen to me, the evil eye would look my way.

Later that evening, as we drank our coffee substitute and

gnawed on the remains of our bread, Rivke told me about the stranger.

"He is Doctor Mengele, the worst of the SS doctors," she said.

I laughed. "He is a Nazi, is there any other kind but the worst?"

"Some doctors actually try to help, but not him. All he is interested in are his experiments."

"What kind of experiments?"

Rivke picked something out of her coffee and took a sip from her bowl. She didn't look at me when she spoke. "He likes twins. He does things with twins, and pregnant women."

I stopped eating. "What kinds of things?"

"Just things, Chana. Do you have to know everything?"

"You know," I said.

"I wish that I did not." She sloshed her drink around in her bowl. "They say he is interested in their brains. He experiments, cuts them open without anesthesia."

"Enough. That is enough," I said. I took what remained of my bread and coffee and organized it into a cloth for my head. I tied the cloth in the back at the base of my head and followed the line to the lavatory huts.

Digging trenches was impossible work. The freezing nights had turned the ground to stone. Our *Kapo* would strut back and forth with whip in hand and an assistant at her side, making sure we were in constant motion. If we weren't fast enough, if our progress wasn't as fast as our neighbors', she would lash out at us with the whip and order the assistants to club us with their sticks.

On that first day out, I made little progress. It was as if I were trying to dig a hole in an iron skillet with a rubber spatula. I tried standing on the shovel and using my weight to break the ground, but I had no weight, none of us did. We were too weak and too light for this kind of work. I looked about me. Were any of the others doing any better? No one seemed to be, so I decided we were safe. I was wrong. The *Kapo* came up behind Matel and watched her work for a few minutes.

"You are getting nowhere," she shouted.

None of us were, but this particular *Kapo* seemed to enjoy picking on her fellow countrywomen, and since she was a Pole, Matel was the perfect target.

Matel rammed the shovel against the ground and threw her body into the handle. She scraped up a puff of dust.

"It will not give." Matel grunted as she tried again to force the earth.

"You lazy Jew!" our Jewish *Kapo* said. "You are worthless. You belong in the chimneys!" She slashed her whip across Matel's back. I rushed over to Matel and grabbed the shovel from her hands. The whip stung at my calves.

"You have your own digging to do, get back over there." The *Kapo* cracked her whip again, first at me and then at Matel.

I tried to jump aside but my coordination was poor. I twisted my ankle and got a lashing on my shoulders. "Wait," I said as I grabbed at my arms and fell to my knees. "Please, when they come to inspect and we have gotten nowhere with the trenches, they will say it is you who is not doing your job."

The *Kapo* stepped in closer. Was she about to kick me? I spoke quickly. "If we can work together we can make the trenches. Let us show you. They will say you are a good *Kapo* if our trenches are the biggest."

She looked down the line at the other groups working, the *Kapos* and assistants behind them.

"Right," she said. She grabbed our left arms, noted our numbers, and motioned for a nearby *Unterkapo* to take them down. "We will have the biggest trenches and if it is not so, you and your young friend here will see the chimneys from the inside tonight." Pleased with her decree, she marched away, her boots smacking the earth as she went.

What had I done? Not only had I made it worse for Matel and myself, but I had also fixed it so our whole party had to work faster and harder if we were to have the largest holes dug in time for inspection that afternoon.

No one said anything to me as we grouped ourselves together and pushed our bodies against the shovels. Rivke and Dvora couldn't even look at me. Bit by bit, layer by layer, we began to scrape up enough of the crust to get our shovels into the moister, softer underground, and the work became a little easier. Still the *Kapo* kept on top of us, leaving the group only long enough to check on another work party's progress. Then she would return to give us her report. It seemed that all the *Kapos* were in on the contest, each interested in having the largest trenches. Word quickly got around to the rest of the prisoners that the young woman down on the other end was the cause of all the extra beatings and the demand for faster, harder work. When our *Kapo* wasn't looking, one of the Russian prisoners from our party came up to me and asked, "Why should we do this for you? What do we care if you burn? I will not kill myself for you."

I knew this was the attitude of everyone there except for Rivke, Dvora, and Matel. When the *Kapos* weren't looking, the work all but stopped. Only the four of us kept working, and I wondered if this weren't perhaps our graves we were digging.

It wasn't until after our soup break in the afternoon that two SS officers, both men, arrived for the inspection. Matel and I had worked so hard in the morning, jumping from trench to trench, lending a hand, trying to keep our section moving, that by afternoon all we could manage were a few scraping motions. We saw our *Kapo* go over to the two men. We watched her explaining something to them. We saw them turn their heads toward us and nod. We watched them as they strode along the line, peering over the edges of the trenches. As they drew nearer, Matel and I worked harder. I could hardly lift the shovel anymore, so I got down on my hands and knees and scratched at the hole. "Please be bigger," I said to myself. "Please be bigger."

One of the officers came up behind me. I kept digging, kept scratching with my fingers. I could feel his feet against my backside. I held my breath.

"So you are the one with the big ideas," he said to me. "Your trench is good." I glanced across at Matel, who was chewing on her lip, her shovel held in midair. "Your *Kapo* can be proud." He paused. I looked over at our *Kapo*, who stood smiling, almost giggling, behind Matel and next to the other officer. I let out my breath. "But it is not the biggest." The officer laughed. Then with his foot he pushed forward against my back, and I tumbled, head first, into the pit. I heard myself cry out, and another voice, quite near, whispered, *"Lord, how long shall I cry and Thou wilt not hear, even cry unto Thee of violence and Thou wilt not save."*

The march back to the camp that afternoon seemed endless. I could not face what I had done. I could not face Matel. I thought of Bubbe and of how hard she had tried to keep me alive, with her food, her warmth, her words. I recalled how often she had told me how important it was for us to survive and to remember, so that when the war was over we could tell people of these atrocities. She counted on them caring, on this being a lesson mankind would only need to learn once, and that their having learned it would redeem the lives of all of us who died here. However, I thought as our enemies did, that few would believe and in time those who did would forget. Besides, I didn't want to be a sacrifice for mankind, and I resented God for creating me if that was my purpose, if that was my reason for existing.

As we approached the gates, I heard the orchestra playing one of their rousing marches. As soon as we were within hearing range of the music, we were supposed to pick up our feet and march through the gates, our gazes forward, arms at our sides.

I didn't care if they beat me a thousand times, I wasn't going to march, I wasn't going to be a part of this game they were playing with the incoming trains. The newcomers would arrive and hear the music, see us marching, and think they were arriving at a real work camp. They, too, would march along, convinced they had finally come to a better place, only to be led to the showers, where they would be locked in, gassed, and then stuffed in the ovens.

As I passed directly in front of the orchestra, I glared at the girl with the cymbals. She looked away. Good, I thought. I had shamed her. I smiled to myself and faced forward. Then I saw in front of me, moving as I moved, my *shvester*. Looking up at her, watching her eyes searching my face, it was I who felt shamed. I was ashamed of my bitterness, my selfishness, and my anger with God. Instead of reaching out, opening myself to others in my suffering the way Bubbe always did, I rejected them, despised their presence, and ended up alone and bitter. Was this the way I wanted the last moments of my life to be?

I switched places in line with Dvora and found myself next to Matel. I took her hand and squeezed it. She squeezed back. "I won't ever let go," I told her. "We'll go up together."

The line dispersed as we reached our block and I pulled Matel forward with the crowd, hoping to get beyond reach of the *Kapo*, but I was not fast enough. She yanked me back by my shirt collar and slammed us both up against the wall of our barracks. Our new *Blockälteste* came forward and the two of them faced away from us and talked. Then the *Kapo* left and the *Blockälteste* stood before us, her legs spread, her hands behind her back. I pulled Matel closer to me and the *Blockälteste* laughed.

"You think you would be selected for making the whole *Kommando* work harder? Eh? You think you would be killed for your trenches?"

We just stood there. She laughed again, and then she walked away.

The next day Matel and I were put on a new *Kommando*, and between us we never again spoke of our death sentence or the day we spent digging trenches.

CHAPTER TWENTY-ONE

Chana

THE DAYS AND NIGHTS grew colder as 1943 ended and the new year began. There were blizzards and ice storms and days when the temperature never got above freezing. There was no heat anywhere except in the SS barracks and headquarters. The rest of us had to stay warm by keeping in constant motion and stuffing organized bits of old newspapers that had been hoarded for use as toilet paper into our shirts. At night when we slept, we stayed warm by packing ourselves together into tight rows of up to seven across. Our shoes and thin clothing protected our modesty but not our bodies. Frostbite and death from exposure were hourly events and, as in the ghetto, I grew adept at stepping over the dead, or almost dead, bodies that lay in the way of my destinations. The energy it would take to go around them, to feel any pity for them, was energy I couldn't spare.

I managed to organize coats for Matel and me by trading some cigarettes I found in a wastebucket stashed behind the lavatory hut. I decided that they had been discarded by prisoners just before they were taken to be gassed, but I didn't think much about that anymore. Cigarettes were valuable currency here. They were used to bribe the guards and officers and to purchase extra food or clothes or spoons.

All of these riches came from a place called *Kanada*, named for that land of plenty that existed far away on the other side of the ocean. This *Kanada* was a storehouse for all the personal belongings the guards tore out of the incoming prisoners' hands, as older prisoners in striped uniforms pulled these victims out of the trains and shoved them into lines.

I had heard stories about the piles of eyeglasses and suit-cases, shoes and blankets, that stood as high as the ceiling in a sorting shed. There were thousands, millions, of photographs, cigarettes, pieces of jewelry, coins, cups, plates, and spoons. The girls who got to work at these sorting sheds were always the best dressed and healthiest looking of all the inmates. They could grab and eat whatever they found hidden in the clothing they sorted, but anything they wanted to bring back to camp they had to smuggle. It cost them their lives if they were caught; but here, just about any slight infraction of the rules cost us our lives. For them, for all of us who risked our lives each day in some small way, it was worth it. Not to take risks was virtual suicide. Any victory we could score against the enemy, no matter how small, was an affirmation of our existence. It was proof that we still had some control over our lives. Taking risks was a necessary part of our survival.

Once or twice a week, I risked my life by using the time before evening *Zählappell*, when all was chaos and commotion, to slip past the guards and go to the *Revier* to see Bubbe. I always found her scurrying toward the back of the barracks in answer to someone's call for water, or bread, or Mama. The hut was just like all the others in the camp, only cleaner, and the bunks were separate pieces of furniture rather than being attached to the walls. Still, the odors that hit me as I entered each time were overwhelming. More than the red cloud that hung over the camp, more than the black smoke in the chimneys, more than the fumes from the lavatory pits, this place smelled — reeked — of death. Selections were made from here more often than any other place, and I feared getting caught in one every time I came. I could not live without my visits with Bubbe, however, so I took the risk whenever I saw the chance.

One afternoon I padded through the snow to her compound, my mind full of distressing news. Bubbe could see at once that I was upset. She found me a chair to sit in and asked one of the orderlies, a prisoner in a striped blue-and-gray uniform, to take over for her.

"Now, Chana, something is wrong with Rivke?" she began.

"Yes, yes, it is true. We had been separated for so long, I didn't know what had become of her but now, now I see her every day. Bubbe, she has been on this *Aussenarbeit* too long. It is killing her. She has to carry these big rocks to the other side of the camp and deliver them to me. I have to watch her struggle across. I see her fall, I see her return each time more cut up, more . . . Bubbe, it is terrible. I cannot watch what they are doing to her. They won't let us trade places. I have to chip the rocks with the hammer; she has to carry them to me. They won't let us trade. She has no fingernails."

Bubbe closed her eyes a moment and then opened them again. "You must tell her to come to me. Tell her to get on the hospital list."

"But, Bubbe, the selections."

"She is safer here. Tell her that. Tell her I will look after her."

I nodded. Someone called out for Bubbe. Even in the *Revier* they called her "grandmother."

Bubbe signaled to the orderly and pulled me up out of my chair. She wrapped her arms around my shoulders and hugged me. "I am proud of you," she said. "I see you are changing. How is Matel?"

I pulled myself out of Bubbe's arms and sat back down. "She is well, I think, but she has lost two toes to frostbite. I need to find a way to get us indoors. I am working on it."

"Good, and Dvora? She is back in your block now, no?"

"Yes, but we do not see her much. To tell you the truth, we do not want to see her."

Bubbe took my face in her hands and studied it. "Dvora has made changes. She is not the same."

I nodded. "I would have expected it from one of the twins but not from her. She has me so confused. She has given me new questions I cannot answer."

"Do not try, Chana."

"Last night I caught her stealing bread out of Marte's arms while she slept, and poor Marte is so ill."

Bubbe squatted down in front of me and ran her hand up my leg. "Is that how you got those bruises?"

I tucked my legs beneath the chair. "I couldn't just let her take it, could I? And I got the beatings. Can you believe? She steals the bread and I get the beatings for waking everyone up. And that is not all. She says wild things, our Dvora. She is not the same girl anymore. She follows the *Blockälteste* around like a puppy, and whispers in my ear at night. The things she says, they frighten me; always in the dark, she leans over me, squeezing my chest and whispering, 'Chana, I have such a plan. Everything will be different for us. We don't belong with these other Jews. We are better than them. You will see. I have a plan.'

"And she's always laughing. Bubbe, I think there is something very wrong with our Dvora."

Bubbe stood up and patted my back. "It is a good idea you

have, to get yourself and Matel inside work. You must do that soon, you must get into another block."

"But we have not been in this one very long, and the *Block-älteste*, she is so much better than the last one we had."

Bubbe's face was dark; her eyes flashed at me like warning lights. I stood up. "Bubbe, what is it?"

Bubbe hugged me and said, "You must go, it will soon be time for *Zählappell*. You do not want to get caught out of your compound."

"But —"

She spun me around and shoved me toward the exit. "Hurry now."

A week later, Rivke was in the hospital under Bubbe's care, but Matel and I were still in the same hut and still working outside with the rocks. Matel was getting so weak that even the extra rations of food I managed to organize did her little good. One morning, when I had to drag her out of the bunk and practically carry her over my shoulders to the lavatory pits, I decided this had to be the day we took the risk and got another work assignment. First, though, we had to get through *Zählappell*.

I did as Dvora and Bubbe had done with me when I was so ill, and stuck her in the back row with me. I didn't even try to stand her up. Heidi, our *Blockälteste*, only checked the back row when the *Lagerälteste* — camp leader and highest-ranking prisoner — or *Rapportführer* was there. She did this for us with the unstated understanding that we would never be late for *Zählappell* or be off in another compound when the whistles blew. All of us made this extra effort, knowing that someday it could be us needing the support of the wall and the cover of the front rows. This morning, Heidi's assistant was too ill to act as her aide and she was sent to the back row with Matel and me.

Those of us who could stood at attention and watched as Heidi marched back and forth in front of us. Every once in a while she'd stop, examine the clipboard she held in her hand, and then begin pacing again. Finally, she turned and pointed at someone three rows back.

"You, step forward," she said.

The woman came forward. It was Dvora, her pet.

"Here, you be my assistant now." Heidi handed Dvora a stick and a red kerchief for her head.

Dvora turned to face us. Her face was red, her eyes wide. Carefully, she bent her head and tied the kerchief around it, then she raised up and gazed out across the sea of prisoners, her prisoners. A wide smile spread across her face.

As soon as the *Lagerälteste* was in sight, Dvora swung her stick at us and shouted, "You can stand up straighter. And you" — her baton came down on someone's head — "where do you think you are, in your living room? Face forward. Be still! Pay attention!" She was certainly earning the extra rations of food her new position would bring her.

When the *Lagerälteste* reached our section, Dvora walked straight up to her and spoke. Heidi was farther down the row, and seeing the two of them talking, she hurried forward, clutching her clipboard to her chest. When she got there, we saw the *Lagerälteste* grab the clipboard out of her hands and smack her over the head with it. The board broke in half.

"Is it true what this girl says? You do favors for the prisoners?" screamed the *Lagerälteste*. She tore Heidi's arm band from her arm and shoved her backward into our lines. She fell to the ground, taking several other women down with her. The

Lagerälteste kicked at her, at all of them, as they scrambled to their feet.

"You know the rules," she bellowed at Heidi. "Everyone must stand at all times during *Zählappell*. If they are too ill to stand, they are too ill to be of any use to the *Reich*. You are lucky it is not Taube here today or you would be stomped to death," she added, still kicking at poor Heidi, who could not get back on her feet. "I will be much nicer to you, however. I will simply put you on the list for Block Twenty-five."

Heidi flung herself at the *Lagerälteste*'s feet. "No!"

The *Lagerälteste* picked up the broken clipboard and handed it to Dvora. "I trust you will do a better job at following the rules, or you, too, will find yourself in the block."

I half expected to see Dvora click her heels and salute. Instead, she took the arm band and the clipboard from the other woman's hands, stepped over Heidi's crouched body, and called us to attention. Her big plan had worked. And why shouldn't it have? I asked myself as I waited out the rest of that *Zählappell*, trying not to catch Dvora's eye. The camp thrived on such back stabbing. The Nazis counted on it. Starving us, working us to exhaustion, and then offering us salvation by giving us charge over our fellow inmates was what kept this giant operation going. It gave us our lives, and it caused our deaths.

After *Zählappell* I brought Matel back into the hut.

"I cannot work today," she said to me as she sagged against the bunks. "Hide me. Hide me under the straw and leave me here."

"But you cannot stay. Dvora has gone mad—who knows what she might do if she finds you. Maybe she'll have you sent off to Block Twenty-five as well."

Tears began to stream down Matel's face. "I hear them screaming at night, in my dreams. At least I think it is in my dreams."

The women in Block Twenty-five were women who had been selected and stripped, if they weren't already, and then taken to the block and locked inside. There they remained until enough women had been selected to fill the gas chamber. This could often take several days, days spent without food or drink.

Matel grabbed my hand. "Sometimes when I hear their screams, I think they're calling to me. I think I hear my name. They're wanting me to go and let them out. I never do. I always hurry past the block whenever I have to go that way. I ignore their cries. They're calling for help and I ignore them. I'm no better than Dvora."

"None of us are, I suppose," I said. "We all want to survive. But that is not likely to happen if Dvora finds you here. Come, we have to go."

"No, please hide me. I will be all right if you can just leave me here."

Against my better judgment, I hoisted Matel onto the top bunk and covered her up with straw. "I will think of you all day," I said. I picked up her hand and kissed it. "Here, take the rest of my bread and eat it at noon. I can think of you then and know you are still alive." I tucked the bread into the palm of her hand. She wrapped her fingers around it and pulled her arm back under the straw. I hopped down and left her there, uncertain if I would ever see her again.

All through the day as I hammered at the chunks of stone delivered to my feet, I worried about Matel. She was so thin, even the assortment of safety pins we had organized could not fasten tight enough to keep her knickers up. If only she could hold out till spring, I told myself; she'd be so much better then. The days were getting warmer and wetter. I felt sure spring was just around the corner.

That afternoon, I was happy to march through the gates to the music and only wished that the orchestra could play faster, so I could reach our compound sooner. At last we were there, and I ran inside and climbed onto the bunk. Matel was not there. I jumped down and climbed onto the next set of bunks. Again she wasn't there. I threw the straw onto the ground and called out to her. She did not answer.

"Are you looking for your daughter, Chana?"

I looked down and saw Dvora smiling up at me.

"What have you done? I will kill you, Dvora. I promise you that." I jumped down off the top bunk and lunged toward her.

She raised her whip and lashed at my wrist. "Is that the way you talk to someone who has just saved Matel's life?"

I wrapped my hand around my wrist. "To Block Twenty-five you have sent her. Is that how you save her?"

"You do not trust me, your friend?"

"I trust no one, especially not you. I will never forget what you did this morning."

"Chana, she is safe." Dvora laughed. "She is on the *Weberei* work unit. I even managed to organize some medicine for her. *She* was not too proud to let me do favors for her, but I wonder, are you?"

"I do not understand."

"I can get you on the unit, too. It is indoor work. You get to sit down. But, of course, if you cannot accept my offer, if you think it would muddy your soul to accept, well, there are others I can help."

"I do not understand."

"Chana, already you said that. It is simple. Do you want to work at the tables with Matel, or do you not?"

"No, I mean, it is you I do not understand. This morning, what you did to Heidi, why did you do that? And now, why do you want to help me?"

"The answer to your first question is simple. I want to survive. The answer to your second question is also simple. I want to help my friends survive. It was my big plan. I told you that. Now we can be safe. Now I can help you."

"I think you want to help me so you can ease your conscience. No, I will not let you off so easy. It should not be so easy. God will not forgive you for Heidi just because you save Matel and help me."

"I thought you did not believe in God," Dvora said, crossing her arms in front of her and letting the whip dangle in her hand.

"No, it is you who does not believe. This morning you turned away from Him, just like the Nazis. You are just the same."

"So, you will not take my offer? Fine. I will send word to Matel."

"No!" I grabbed her arm as she turned away. She wrenched her arm out of my grip, but she stopped.

"Well?" she said.

I looked down at the ground of our hut, already turning to spring mud. "I'd like to go," I said.

"What?"

"You heard what I said, Dvora."

"But I did not hear the magic words."

"Please," I said.

"Please, what?"

"Please, Dvora, can I go to the *Weberei* unit?"

Dvora laughed. "You are not so different from me, young Chana." Then she turned and left the hut.

I didn't know if Dvora was really going to switch me over to the new unit until after *Zählappell* the next morning, when a woman with a swollen face and scarlet cheeks came by and called out my number. As I followed her out of the compound, past the lines marching off to *Aussenarbeit*, I felt my heart jump. At last I was going to work inside, and I had Dvora to thank for it. However, I wasn't going to think about that. I wasn't going to think at all, and I hoped, with all my heart, that I would never see Dvora again.

CHAPTER TWENTY-TWO

Chana

MOST OF THE SPRING of 1944 was cold and ugly, but every once in awhile, a day would come when the sun would be strong enough to break through the thick red sky and warm the ground beneath our feet. On days like that, *Zählappell* was almost bearable, and during our midday break, when we received our bowl of *Lagersuppe*, we could sit out on the ground and feel the heat seeping through our flesh, thawing out our bones.

Our work on the *Weberei* unit was tedious but not back breaking. We sat at long tables piled high with rags and paper as stiff as wood. We tore them into strips with our hands and braided them, often tearing the skin off our hands as well. Every day we had to complete a rope of twenty meters, and it had to be strong enough so that when the SS came around and tried to pull it apart, it held tight. These ropes were used for throwing hand grenades, so their strength was most important. If they fell apart, or if our daily quota was not met, the *Kapos* would beat us and threaten us with selection.

Although we were now indoors, Matel's recovery was slow. There was so little food to give her strength, so little time for rest, and because of her inability to work up to speed, she was often beaten.

Watching her struggle, trying to control her shivering as

she lay in my arms at night, her arms and legs like smoldering embers, I could only marvel at her inner strength, her fierce will to survive.

All day, I prayed for God to make her well. I began again my old practice, long ago enforced by Bubbe and Zayde, where everything I said, everything I did, was to honor and thank God. My work was excellent and was often held up for others to see. My own health and strength improved daily. Even the SS seemed to respect me because I had survived so well and for so long. I was one of the "old numbers" now.

All of this I did in the hopes that God would send His healing from heaven, so Matel could get well.

Finally, as late spring's warmth gave way to summer's heat, I began to see an improvement in Matel. First it was just her eyes, no longer so feverish and glassy; and then her cough, which sounded so dry and hollow, faded to short and occasional barks. I knew she was going to make it, and together we thanked God for His power to heal a body and soul so sick and tortured.

One night after we had climbed into our bunk, Matel rolled over to face me and said, "Let's have a ceremony."

"A ceremony? Here? I think, Matel, your fever has returned."

"We need to thank God officially. We can pretend it is a holiday. Please, Chana. We hardly know what day it is anymore. The only time we know it is a Jewish holiday is when Mengele shows up for selections."

Genia, a girl of only sixteen, hung her head over the top bunk. "He is our Jewish calendar." She laughed. Then more seriously, "I would come to your ceremony, Matel."

"Me, too," came whispers from above and below.

"But you are not completely healed. Perhaps we should

wait." There was silence. "All right, when?" I asked. "When shall we do it?"

Everyone put forth suggestions, for not only when to do it, but how, and what needed to be organized, and who was to say and do what.

It was a crazy thing to attempt in a place like this. Those of us who gathered in the center of the hut that evening to make plans knew that the chances of all of us even surviving until the night of the ceremony were unlikely. Selections were being made more frequently than ever. Trains arrived day and night now, with thousands of men, women, and children being unloaded and sent straight to the crematoria. The chimneys smoked continuously, and everywhere, always, the sky was red. Still, never had we felt more alive, more close and supportive of one another than we did during that week of preparation; and young Matel was in charge of it all. She spent every spare moment she had hunting down items, organizing them, planning and coordinating the big event.

Over the next several days we smuggled extra pieces of the tough paper used to make our ropes out of the work shed. We carried these strips in our armpits or stuffed them around the toes of our clogs and at night braided them together to make candles. We ran around to the back of the kitchen barracks and collected extra scraps of food from the rubbish heaps. Anything — onion skins, wilted cabbage leaves, potato shavings, with their promise of extra life-sustaining vitamins — was used to trade for extra bread. Genia's sister worked in the *Kanada Kommando* and was able to pass along some matches and a beautiful red, blue, and yellow shawl.

At last we had all the things we needed for our ceremony. We waited until night, when the *Blockälteste* had gone to her own room at the end of the block. The sky was black. Rain was falling and we could hear it beating down on the roof of the hut. Thunder cracked above us in the sky. Matel and several of the others dug up our cache of goodies, which we had buried in the ground inside our hut, while I hurried to the two windows and tucked a piece of dark green material around the edges of each so no light could be seen. Then I lit our first homemade candle. I carried it in my bowl over to our circle. Those who were too ill to participate, or who just wanted to watch, looked out from their bunks as we recited the blessing for the lighting of the candles. Then one by one our candles were lit. Flickering flames of light and shadow filled the hut. I raised my voice above the sound of the heavy beating of the rain and said, "We light these candles tonight as a symbol of peace and freedom, and of the light which this night brings to our souls." Thunder rolled across the sky above us. We drew in closer, forming a tight circle, and together repeated, "We light these candles tonight as a symbol of peace and freedom, and of the light which this night brings to our souls." Then everyone placed their pieces of bread on the colorful shawl that was spread out in the center of the circle. More thunder sounded above. We held one another's hands as we recited in unison, "Blessed are You, Lord our God, King of the Universe, who brings forth bread from the earth." I could hear the others behind me in their bunks whispering with us, and as we sat in silence eating our bits of bread, they, too, ate theirs.

During the meditation that followed, I listened to the rain and watched the candles curling in our bowls. Then Matel stood up and moved around the outside of our circle and in a thin voice, peppered with coughs, sang, "I will extol Thee, O Lord, for Thou hast drawn me up, and have not allowed my foes to rejoice over me. O Lord, My God, I cried out to Thee, and Thou didst heal me. O Lord, Thou raised my soul from the grave, Thou kept me alive that I should not descend to the pit."

Then I stood up and joined Matel on the outside of the circle. Together we moved around it, and I said, "What profit is there in my blood if I die? Can the dust give thanks to Thee? Can it declare Thy truth?"

Over the sound of the rain and the thunder we heard the screech of a train braking to a stop outside. We heard the whistles and dogs barking and officials shouting. I prayed for more thunder to drown out the sounds.

I motioned for everyone to stand up, and again we held hands and circled around the cloth and our bowls of candles left on the ground. Together we recited the last lines of the psalm: "Thou hast turned for me my mourning into dancing; Thou hast opened my sackcloth, and girded me with gladness. So that my soul may sing praise to Thee, and not be silent; O Lord, my God, I will give thanks unto Thee forever."

I had thought I couldn't cry anymore. I had thought all feelings and emotions had died in me long ago, but as we stood swaying in our circle, squeezing one another's hands and watching the last of the candles flicker, glow, then die, I felt the tears spilling down my cheeks, and I looked up to the ceiling and laughed.

The next morning, after our long night, the whistles seemed to blow even earlier than usual, and all of us had a hard time rousing ourselves. Our *Blockälteste* stormed in and shouted, "*Alles, Stehen Sie auf—zum Zählappell!*"

I moaned and shook Matel. "Get up, come on, the beast has spoken." She did not answer. She did not move. I shook her again, but I knew it was useless. Her body was cold and hard. Matel was dead.

The *Blockälteste* stormed in and cracked me on the head. "Did you not hear the whistles? Get up!" She looked down at Matel and then back at me. "Get up or you will be dragged out to the piles with her." She yanked my arms forward and I tumbled out of the bunk. "Stand up, you stupid rag." She got behind me, grabbed me from under my arms, and scooted me out the door. Then she blocked the way so I could not go back in.

I stood on the outside of my row during *Zählappell* that morning, not caring that it was the worst place to stand if you wanted to avoid getting beaten. It was still raining, and Matel was dragged by her feet out of the hut and through the mud that squished around our ankles. They piled her up with the other dead bodies at the end of our row, and I stood beside her praying that *Zählappell* would last all day.

Whenever I could, I'd sneak a glance at her. I'd catch her face with its summer freckles running across the bridge of her nose, or get a peek at her wrist, skinny like a baby's rattle, and I'd try to reach down and touch her. Her long body lay tangled with the others near the top of the heap. She had been dragged partway out of her knickers and her blouse was hiked up above her rib cage. Every time I made a move toward her, the *Block-älteste* or her assistant would come to club me on the back and shoulders.

Zählappell lasted only three hours that day, and when it was over I could not leave.

Genia and her friend Zocha came up to me.

"Chana, you must come. You cannot be late," Genia said. The two of them pulled me away from Matel.

Already the *Leichenkommando* were removing the bodies.

"Wait, please, one second," I said, and before they could get a tighter grip, I pulled free and ran back to the pile. I lifted

Matel's leg out from under the body beneath her and pulled up her knickers. Then I pulled her shirt down and tried to tuck it in. A man from the *Leichenkommando* came up behind me, and I turned around to face him. "She was my—my . . . She was mine."

His face was blank, his eyes unseeing. I knew he didn't understand, but my *shvester*, standing beside him, did.

Weeks later, a messenger girl with red spikes of hair shooting up from her head and a slight hunch in her shoulders was waiting for me at the entrance to the *Weberei* shed.

"You play the violin?" she asked me.

"Yes."

"You play it well?"

"I would not say I play if I did not play it well," I replied.

"*Gut*, come with me."

"Where, what do you mean?"

"This is your lucky day. You will join the orchestra."

"What?"

"Yes." She nodded, her neck dipping like a goose. "It is so. Follow me."

This couldn't be true. It was too much. I would never play in Hitler's orchestra, never, no matter what they did to me.

"Come!" she said, when she saw that I hadn't moved.

I looked behind me. The *Kapo* was standing there nodding.

"You must go," the *Kapo* said. "It is a good thing, you will see."

"I do not want your favors," I replied.

The *Kapo* glanced at the messenger girl and then spit on the ground. "You think I do favors for you? Never, you stupid fool. Go!" She shoved me forward into the messenger girl's arms.

I followed the girl to the music block. *Shvester* was with me. She had been with me ever since Matel's death. She was my only companion now. I stayed away from everyone else, making no new friends and ignoring my old ones. I hadn't been able to see Bubbe since moving to the *Weberei* unit because it was too far away from the *Revier* to risk visiting before *Zählappell*. I didn't even know if she knew about Matel. I didn't even know if she was still alive, and I couldn't bear to find out.

Stepping into the music hut was like stepping into a dream where fairy-tale images intertwined with the macabre. In the center of the room stood a woman on a platform, facing a collection of girls, all neatly dressed in dark pleated skirts and white blouses with striped jackets. Their bodies and faces were scrubbed clean and each one held an instrument in her hands. There were violins, mandolins, guitars, flutes, pipes, drums, cymbals, and over to one side, a grand piano. There were light bulbs turned on, hanging from the ceiling, and at one end of the room were bunk beds with real mattresses and wool blankets pulled up over them. The floor beneath my feet was wooden and clean, the walls white. There was a stove over near the dining section with a pot of water heating on it, and just outside, just a few yards away from the entrance to this fairyland, was the end of the Birkenau railway. From where I stood, I could turn my head one way and watch hundreds of people hunched and ashen spilling out of cattle cars, the dead bodies that curled around their feet being tossed into a nearby pit. Then I could turn my head the other way and watch young women, warm and clean, sitting in a white room, their feet neatly placed together, instruments in their hands.

They were practicing "The Blue Danube" when I entered.

The woman on the platform stopped conducting when she saw me, and the music stopped. She stepped down off the platform and I saw that she was a short woman, with broad shoulders and a thick waist.

"You are our violinist?" she asked me.

I nodded.

She went over to a long table covered with papers and scores and picked up the violin lying there. She handed it to me.

"Play," she said.

"What shall I play?"

"Whatever you want. Whatever you know."

I thought a moment. Did I know anything anymore? I recalled the piece by Schumann that Tata and I had worked on for the orchestra in Poland. One Sunday, just two days before my audition, we had practiced the solo section the entire day, arguing over every aspect of my interpretation of the piece. By the end of the day, I was in tears and Tata was slamming doors, his face purple with frustration. Mama was so mad at both of us she locked us in the pantry together, without music or instruments, and told us to just talk. We argued over the music for less than five minutes and then spent the evening crouched in that small space, discussing our dreams, our fears, and my future. How I wished now that I could relive that day.

I tucked the violin under my chin. It had been years since I had done that, and yet it felt right, as if I had done it just hours ago. I plucked at the strings. It had been tuned recently, but still I readjusted the tuning pegs and ran my bow across the strings a few times. It was a way of making the instrument mine, of reacquainting myself with an old friend. I looked out at the group of girls sitting in front of me, most of them about my age or younger, their instruments resting in their laps or against their chests. A few of them smiled. I smiled back, not at them, but at *Shvester*. I turned to the conductor.

"I will play the solo in Schumann's 'Reverie.'"

I shrugged my shoulders to reposition the violin, raised my bow, and played the first few measures. Yes, I remembered it! I closed my eyes and let the music flow out of me, my fingers moving with a memory all their own. When I was through, the girls all applauded — all except one.

"She looks terrible," said the girl. "If we took a week we could never get her cleaned up enough."

"I think she's very ill," said another, as if I weren't even there. Then they all started in on me.

"She would be selected for sure if she played on Sunday."

"She's being eaten alive with lice. She might have typhus, look at all those sores."

"She doesn't even have any shoes or socks."

"She's way too thin and her head has bald patches. They won't want to be watching her. Claire is right, she will be selected."

"She looks too Jewish."

I had let all of their comments just wash right over me — what did I care what they thought? I didn't want to be in their orchestra — but this last comment startled me. I looked up and noticed for the first time that the chairs were grouped together into two sections. Jews were sitting on the left and non-Jews on the right. This had to be the only block where they allowed non-Jews to work alongside Jews.

The orchestra leader waved her hand. "We can clean her up, you will see. And she will be wearing different clothes, and a scarf over her head like the rest of you. It will work out."

"If Alma were still alive she would not take her," said an

enormous girl who looked as if she had eaten an entire warehouse of food.

The conductor slammed her baton down on the girl's music stand. "Alma would take her because she is a good musician, unlike most of you here; and anyway, I am the conductor now, I am your *Kapo*." She turned back to me. "You can take a seat over there." She pointed her baton at a chair in the front of the other violinists.

I hesitated.

"Don't worry. We take showers here every day. You will be ready by Sunday," she said.

We rehearsed all day, breaking only for our midday meal. In this strange place the *Lagersuppe*, with its foul odor and sickening taste, was the only thing familiar to me.

We repeated the same simple phrase over and over, until everyone could play it correctly and up to tempo. Then we'd move on to the next phrase and do the same thing. When we returned to the music the next day it was as if most of the girls had never seen the music before, and again we repeated each phrase a hundred times until it was correct.

It wasn't all our fault, however. I soon realized that Sonia, our conductor, was not very good at her job. She tried to cover it up with a lot of knuckle slamming with her baton, but she left me alone. Everyone did. They didn't know what to make of me, and for the first three days I moved from place to place in a kind of trance. The existence of this block in this camp was beyond my comprehension. We took our showers daily with warm water and soap, and dried ourselves off with towels. I got not only a clean skirt and blouse to wear, but also a bra, underwear, dark stockings, and real shoes. We had to stand for *Zählappell*, but it was indoors, inside the hut. The only time we ever went outside at all was to go to the lavatory, the showers, or to play for the workers as they marched through the gate.

It was during the morning of my fourth day there that Sonia came up to me and told me I was to play for the workers that morning.

My *shvester* was standing by my side when I shook my head and told Sonia I wouldn't play outside.

"You will play or go up the chimney."

"But I cannot. To play and cause someone to fall, or force someone to hurry who can't even pick up her legs so that the dogs are set upon her and she is eaten alive, I cannot do."

Sonia smacked my wrist with her baton. "Where do you think you are? You are not at home. You have no choice unless you want to die. Do you? Is that why you look as you do? Is that why you act as you do?"

All these months I had been here in the prison camp fighting with all I had to stay alive, fighting to keep from becoming a *Muselmann*, only to come full circle. Again I was questioning everything, again I was trying to make sense out of nonsense, reason out of no reason.

The girls were gathering up their instruments and filing out of the hut.

"Well, what is your answer?"

I went over to my chair, put on my jacket, picked up my violin, and followed the others outside. It was simple — no need for questions or reasons; more than anything, I wanted to live.

Chana

I NEVER GOT USED to playing for the workers. I refused to look at them as they marched in front of our platform each morning and again each night, but I could feel their hate, their misery. I wanted to throw down my violin, run down to the line, and march along with them. I wanted to tell them, "I'm with you; I belong with you," but I didn't have the courage. If it weren't for the warmth of the music block, the comfort of having my own bed with a mattress and blanket, and the daily showers, I never would have survived. I was sick, spending many a morning and evening before *Zählappell* with my face over a lavatory hole.

Although I could see Bubbe almost every Sunday now, she could do little to help me. Either before or after our Sunday concerts, which nurses and doctors and even some prisoners were allowed to attend, Bubbe and I would exchange hurried tidbits of information. She told me about Rivke dying, and I told her about Matel. A few times she managed to hand me a couple of pills, instructing me to take them right away, but they were never enough for a cure.

One Sunday, I was feeling so ill, I pleaded with Bubbe to let me go to the *Revier*.

"No, not now. Now is the worst time. They are making

selections at the hospital daily. If you can still walk, it is best you stay where you are."

"But what is happening? Why are the Germans so jumpy all of a sudden?"

"The Allies are advancing. The war could be over any day. Think of it, we could be liberated any day now."

Her words were full of hope, but her eyes were not.

"I fear they will not let us survive," I said. "The Germans will kill us all before they surrender to the Allies."

Bubbe grabbed my hands and closed her eyes. "Just hold on, Chana. Please hold on."

I tried to do as Bubbe said, tried to hold on, but my body was refusing to cooperate. Our daily ritual of seventeen hours of practice had become unendurable, my fingers fumbling on the strings, my left arm trembling as I tried to keep the violin in position.

One afternoon, as we were going over "The Charge of the Light Brigade" for the thousandth time that day, my feet slid out from under me, and I felt myself slip out of the chair and onto the floor. The next thing I knew, I was on top of my bed and Eleni, a pretty Greek girl, was bending over me.

"I am supposed to see if you are all right now," she said in a monotone.

I sat up. "Yes, sorry."

"If Alma were here, she'd send you to the *Revier*. It is not fair, your special privileges."

"If I went to the *Revier* now, I would be selected for sure."

Eleni nodded. "Yes."

"So that is why I am here."

"My sister was selected from the *Revier*," she said, still in her monotone.

"Yes, that is why I am here," I repeated.

"Why should you be so special, Jew girl? Because you are an old number? That is no reason."

"Because I am a human being."

She laughed. "That is nothing here."

I watched her pick up her violin from the foot of my bed. When she tucked it under her arm, a glint of gold caught my eye. She turned to leave.

"Wait," I called her back. "That is — that is my violin! I do not believe it, you have my violin!" I popped up from the bed and the room spun around. I fell back onto the bed.

"This is my violin," she said. "Your violin is back at your seat, where you should be if you will not go to the *Revier*."

"No, you do not understand, that is mine. Those are my initials on the back, C.S. See the gold letters on the neck? My tata had it made for me. That is mine!"

Eleni grabbed the violin by its neck and backed away. "You are sick. You do not know if this is yours. You are sick, stupid Jew." She turned and ran back to the other side of the hut.

I tried everything I could think of to get Eleni to trade violins with me, but it gave her too much pleasure to see me so miserable; she would never hand it over to me. Whenever she caught me looking at her, at the violin, she'd pretend to bang it accidentally against her stand, or into a chair. She'd tighten the strings so much they'd pop, and when she was through for the day, she'd wait until I was looking her way and toss the instrument into its case. She used the case to rest her muddy feet on, claiming that it made her uncomfortable to sit in a chair with her feet dangling for so many hours.

I felt guilty for feeling so upset about my violin. I was being childish, I told myself. What did a silly wooden case with some strings matter compared to what was going on all around me? However, everyone that fall was on edge. We felt certain that each day was going to be our last.

At night we could hear planes flying overhead and we knew they weren't the usual run of Messerschmitts. These planes belonged to the Allies, and the bomb drops were getting closer.

The Germans worked at a frantic pace. The crematoria were no longer able to burn all the people who were gassed each day, so they began tossing them into ravines, dousing them with benzine — not even bothering to kill them first — and setting them on fire.

From my bed at night I could hear tortured screams intermingled with the distant bombs, and all I could do was shiver beneath my blanket and pray.

During the day, a *Lagersperre* could last up to six hours, while the SS made their selections. When it was over the SS would often come to the music hut to relax, expecting us to play for them, to help them unwind.

Usually it was the *Lagerführerin*, head of the women's camp, and *Herr Kommandant* Krammer, commandant of Birkenau, who came to hear us play. They were the true music lovers of the camp, the reason the music hut existed in the first place. But one day, after a four-hour *Lagersperre*, Dr. Mengele and *Rapportführer* Taube came strutting into our hut. Taube looked drunk. He kept knocking into Mengele as they made their way to the seats behind the conductor's platform.

"*Singen! Singen!*" Taube ordered.

Sonia bowed to the two men, turned around to face us, and signaled for us to rise. We went through our usual repertoire of German folk songs, but I could not sing. I could feel myself mouthing the words but nothing would come out. I could not perform for these two men.

I don't know if Taube could tell I was not singing, or if he recognized me from before, but when the songs were over he called me forward. I patted down my skirt, licked my lips, and stepped up next to the platform.

"You play the violin?"

I nodded.

"Then play. Play me some — some Bach."

I couldn't think of any piece to play. I couldn't remember anything. I suddenly wasn't even sure I knew how to play the violin anymore. I stared down at the bow in my hand and wondered which way to hold it. I looked up at Taube. He had taken several steps toward me. I could see his bloodshot eyes. He clenched his teeth, his lips pressed up against his gums. I twisted away just as he raised his rifle and rammed it into the back of my skull.

"Play!" he growled as I fell forward onto my knees and then down onto my face.

My head was reeling, the floor beneath me seemed to be tilting, then dissolving, and then tilting again. I could feel something warm moving down the back of my head.

"Play!" Taube repeated.

I got up onto my hands and knees and crawled forward. I searched the faces of all the girls sitting before me for my *shvester*, but she was gone. When I needed her most, she was gone.

Dear God, I prayed, *be with me*.

I found myself kneeling in front of Eleni. I gazed up into her eyes, my mouth open. I tried to speak. She leaned forward, grabbed my arms, and pulled me up off the floor. Then she handed me her violin, my violin, and turned me around to face my audience. "Play, Chana," she whispered. "Play for your tata."

I closed my eyes and I played my violin. I played Bach's "Chaconne," and when I was through everyone stood up and applauded. They rushed toward me and formed a line; they all wanted to shake my hand. I stepped forward and thanked each person there: Tata, Mama, Zayde, Anya, Mosze, Jakub, Matel, Rivke, Mr. Hurwitz, Mrs. Hurwitz, Mr. Krengiel, Mrs. Krengiel, Mrs. Liebman — I stopped.

"How long is this line?" I asked Mrs. Liebman.

"It never ends," she replied.

Chana

"TAUBE MUST HAVE ASSUMED you were dead," Bubbe told me when I came to in the *Revier*. "He told Sonia to leave you for the *Leichenkommando*."

I ran my hand down the back of my head. Bubbe had sewn it up and the thick bits of thread felt strange beneath my hand.

"I will be selected," I said. "Maybe they should have left me for dead."

Bubbe shook her head. "Everything is upside down. Even the Germans don't know what they are doing. The whole camp is being evacuated. The music block has been cleared, they are gone."

"Gone?"

Bubbe nodded.

I tried to imagine the hut empty, the instruments left on the chairs. Where had they been taken? Were they still alive? I remembered my dream, my vision of all my dead friends and family lined up in front of me. Would they be in that line now? I told Bubbe what I had seen. I told her that Mama and Anya and Jakub were in that line.

"I am sorry, Chana."

"But it does not mean they are dead, does it? I was just dreaming."

"You have the gift," she said.

"Your gift?"

"Yes."

Someone from another bunk called for water, and Bubbe left me.

I thought about her gift. She knew so much. She knew people so well. She could read their lives, past and future. She could understand them and love them, all of them. I was not like that.

When she returned to my side I said to her, "I do not have your gift. I cannot see the future, I cannot read people the way you do."

"You are young yet, give it time."

"But I am not sure I want such a gift. I see how it has been a burden to you."

"Someday, Chana, you will be able to use it to help someone, to save someone's life. Then it will be a gift."

I thought about that for a moment and then said, "There was this girl, I called her my *shvester*. I could see her, she was so real, but I think she was a—a gift."

Bubbe nodded. "Yes, a different kind of gift. All of us here have that kind of gift in one form or another. It is how we survive. It is how we cope."

"But who was she?"

"She was you, Chana. She was the brave Chana, the strong Chana, the Chana who could cry and mourn so many deaths, so much destruction, so that you wouldn't have to. To pity yourself, or anyone else, is to die here—you know that. But to feel nothing, it is death to the soul. Your *shvester*, your other self, kept your soul alive; and you, you have kept your body alive.

"Yes, it is good you had this *shvester*, but she is gone now, yes?"

I nodded. "She will not be coming back."

Bubbe smiled. "You will find something better."

"What do you mean?"

Bubbe opened her mouth to speak, but she was stopped by a voice coming from the entrance of the hut.

"Anyone who can walk must come out. Hurry! Get up! Get up!"

I could hear others moving. I tried to get up but Bubbe pushed me back down. "No, you must stay here."

"But I have to go with you." I looked in her eyes. "Bubbe, please."

She leaned over and kissed both my cheeks. "You will be all right," she said. "You have all you need. And Chana, remember. Remember all of this."

Bubbe turned away. I tried to get up and follow her, but my feet wouldn't hold my weight. "But I need you," I called after her. "I need you!"

I don't know how many days I spent moving in and out of consciousness. I was aware of someone feeding me, giving me lots of water, wrapping me in layers of warm blankets. Once, I woke to find Dvora huddled over me, the back of her hand resting on my cheek.

"The place is deserted," she said. "There are just a few of us still here. I have found a whole storehouse of food, so don't worry, I can take care of you until the Russians come."

"It will be too late when they get here; I cannot hold out."

Dvora forced some more water down my throat. "Don't give up, Chana. I am here to care for you."

"I thought I never wanted to see you again," I said. "How is it you are here?"

"I have been here for several weeks on the dysentery block. Bubbe took care of me. She saved my life."

I nodded and fell back beneath my blankets and closed my eyes. I felt my body begin to spin forward. I tried to open my eyes so I could see. I began to dream. I began to see things. I could see Bubbe taking care of Dvora, and Dvora taking care of me, and I was taking care of Matel, and Matel was taking care of her mother, and on it continued, branching out to the left and right, and then weaving and looping back around into a circle so great I could only view the merest fraction of it. And marching through this circle was the line of dead friends I had seen before, only this time, Bubbe was leading it.

I ran up to Bubbe and I asked her, "What is the meaning of this?"

"You know," she said.

I stepped back and looked at all the people as they continued to weave in and out, around and around, faster and faster until they were one blur, until they were One. And then I knew what Bubbe meant. Here, was God.

When I opened my eyes again I was staring up at a funny-looking man wearing a long overcoat and a peculiar cap with a red star on the front.

He stood watching me a moment.

I blinked.

"Dear God," he said in Russian. "She's alive!"

CHAPTER TWENTY-FIVE

Hilary

I'M SPINNING. I can hear sounds and voices all around me. I hear sirens like a high-pitched humming in my ears. Louder than the sirens are the sounds of glass chinking, metal on metal, air whooshing, and louder and closer still, the voices.

. . . We're losing her, Doctor . . . can't get a reading . . . hold it steady . . . come on, fight, little lady . . . more blood . . . can't . . . heartbeat . . .

The voices stop. I'm spinning—forward. All around me is dark except a pinpoint of light in the distance. I begin to spin toward the light and it spreads out before me until the whole space is bright light. I can see someone standing in front of me. Someone I know.

"Grandma?"

"Yes."

"You're speaking to me."

"Now you are ready to listen."

"But who are you?"

"You know."

"I— Yes—I think—yes! You're Chana! But you don't look well. You're dying."

"You have changed, Hilary."

"Yes. I know things now. I understand."

"Bubbe used to say to me, 'If you can understand a person, you can love him.' "

"Yes, I remember."

"What else do you remember?"

"I remember it all. It's my life, too, now. You and me, we share the same past."

"Yes, Hilary, we all do. Everyone shares the same past, the same future, but some will see it better than others."

"Like Bubbe and her gift. And you. It's through the gift that I've been able to live this other life, your life."

"Yes. It was you Bubbe meant when she said that I would someday use my gift to save someone's life."

"That was so long ago."

"No, just a thought away."

"Chana . . ."

"I must leave now, Hilary."

"No! Wait! What am I supposed to do now?"

"Use what you know to change things. You can change the world, Hilary."

"No. I can change me, but nothing else. Things— The world has always been this way. What difference could I make? What difference did you make?"

"I reached out to you. I touched you. I screamed, and you heard. You are a witness. It is your turn to remember, and to tell, and to keep on telling until you are sure others have heard."

"You're asking too much. I don't have your gift. How can I reach anyone? Who will listen to me? I'm not even Jewish."

"You were an Aryan Warrior, a Neo-Nazi. People will listen. Students will listen. Your past will be your gift."

"I'm afraid. I don't think I can do what you ask of me. I can't go back."

"You have to. You are a part of the chain, Hilary. We are

connected now. In hearing me, in understanding me, you have given my past new meaning. It will change the meaning of your past as well, and someday your life as an angry child who has turned her hate to love will change still another life. You're a part of the chain, one you cannot break."

"But I'm afraid it will all be the same if I go back. Nothing will have changed."

"*You* have changed. That is all that matters."

"I can't go back."

"You won't be alone."

"You will be there with me?"

"No, not I."

"You mean God? Chana, you're fading. Chana? No, don't leave. Don't leave! I'm going with you. I will not do as you say. I will not go back. I can't do it."

"You will be all right. I have done my job, now it is your turn."

"No, I'm afraid. Don't leave! Chana? I'm coming with you. Please!"

I stare out into the light. A face comes into view. I blink.

"Dear God, she's awake. Nurse, she's awake! Look, she's awake!"

"There now, didn't I tell you?" The nurse hovers over me. All I can see is her mouth.

"You gave us all quite a scare, young lady. Do you know where you are?"

"I— In bed?"

"Yes." She laughs. "What's your name?"

"I have—I have two names."

"Yes! Yes, that's right. Hilary Burke!"

"Mrs. Burke, we prefer to let Hilary answer the questions. Now, do you know who this is?"

"Yes — Mama?"

"That's right, good."

"She's never called me that before."

"Please, Mrs. Burke. Honey, do you know what year it is?"

"I know — It's after the — the war. The war is over."

"The war? What does she mean? Nurse, is she going to be all right?"

"She's still a bit confused, but don't worry, Mrs. Burke, it's very normal."

A finger is placed in front of my face.

"Do you see my finger?" the nurse asks.

"Yes."

"Good. Now I want you to follow it with your eyes."

I follow her finger back and forth, up and down, all the while watching the back of her long nail.

"That was very good. Do you feel this?"

"Ouch!"

"Very good! I think your daughter's going to be just fine. We'll get Dr. Bernstein in here."

"Can I talk to her now?"

"Go right ahead, but she may not remember what you say. She's still pretty groggy."

Mama leans into the bed. All I can see are her eyes, round and blue, with pieces of old mascara clinging to her lashes.

"Hilary — All I — Thank God."

"Mama?"

"Yes."

"You're here."

"Yes. I couldn't leave you. That's what I wanted to say. I wanted to say — to say, well, baby, I — I love you."

"I know."

"You do?"

"You stayed with me — through the fire."

"How did you know? How could you know? That happened yesterday."

"Brad's fire."

"How can you know that?"

"They kept trying to make you leave — a real fire."

"It's a wonder the whole building didn't burn down. They even had to evacuate the other wing."

"But — you stayed."

"Yes, but how do you know all this? And what about Brad?"

"I — don't — Simon."

"Yes, baby. Simon's missing."

"How long?"

"Three days. You've been out three days."

"You stayed."

"Yes."

I close my eyes and sleep. I dream that I'm trapped in the room above the ceiling with Simon. It's so hot we're suffocating. We scream but no one hears.

Mama is staring at me when I open my eyes.

"It's okay, baby, you just had a bad dream."

"Simon. I know — where."

"Shh."

"I know where he is."

"Hilary, what do you mean? You know where Simon is?"

"The hole."

"A hole? He's in a hole?"

"Yes."

"Good Lord! Nurse, nurse! We need you! Where is this hole? Hilary, can you remember? We need to find him. The nurse can call the police. Just tell us where he is, baby."

"The ghetto."

"Oh, nurse, that missing child, she knows where he is. Hilary, what's the ghetto? Is that a hangout? A restaurant? Oh, the police will know. Please, nurse, could somebody call them? Tell them the missing boy's in a hole at the ghetto.

"You sleep now, baby. Sleep now."

"Simon—I must find . . ."

"Shh, sleep now. We'll find him."

"He's in a hole. No! No, he's—he's in a locker."

"Hilary, think. Is he in a hole or in a locker?"

"Mrs. Burke, let her rest. It's still too soon."

"Yes, yes, I'm sorry. I just thought she knew. It seemed like she knew."

"I know where."

"Shh—it's okay, baby."

"Listen to me!"

"Now, look, she's all upset. Mrs. Burke—"

"The gym locker! Simon is there."

"Hilary, are you sure?"

"Mrs. Burke!"

"Brad, and Chucky, and Billy."

"Okay, baby. You sleep. Everything will be all right. Everything will be all right. Sleep now."

I close my eyes. I hear Mama's voice whispering to me again and again, "Everything will be all right." I feel her hand on my head, her breath on my cheek. I drift off to sleep and dream of baby Simon playing patty-cake with my father.

When I open my eyes, I see that I'm wrapped in white. My left leg is in a cast suspended from a stirrup. Mama is still here sitting beside me. Her face is pale and small, too small for all her hair. She is frowning at her hands, studying them. Her Bible is about to slide off her lap.

"Mama, what is it? Is Simon . . . ?"

"Oh, Hilary." She catches her Bible. "Yes, they found him. It's all over."

"Tell me, I want to know."

"Another time."

"I want to know. It's all right, Mama."

"No, it can wait. Let's get you well."

"Please!"

"It's not good."

"I know. The police, they'll want to talk to me. I'll tell them."

"Baby, Brad and the others, they're in jail."

"Where is Simon? Is he — is he dead?"

"The police found him in back of the school."

"But how . . ."

"It was Brad, baby. Brad hung him up by his suspenders. In a tree. He told the poor kid if his suspender buttons broke, he'd shoot him. Chucky and Billy were there, too, teasing him, threatening him."

"He's dead! He's dead! I remember. They shot him hanging in the tree!"

"No. No, Hilary. He's all right. He's here. Down on the second floor. It's okay. The kid did okay. He's alive. He found a water bottle in that locker, three-quarters full, and some orange peels. He's okay. He'll be okay."

"He's really . . ."

"I promise."

"And you. You stayed with me."

"Yes, baby, I'm here. Things are going to be better. I promise, things will be better."

"I know, Mama."

She moves closer. I feel her lips on my forehead.

I close my eyes and sleep, and dream about a grown man hanging in a tree and a woman named Chana.

People bustle in and out of my room at all hours of the day and night wanting to run tests, to take me to therapy, to feed me, to medicate me, and even to visit me, but never does a gray old woman named Chana come to see me.

I begin to wonder, Who is this woman who haunts my sleep, who tells me incredible things, expects incredible things of me? Why do I know her so well? Why do I feel this pull on me from somewhere else? Why do I want to be with her so much, when I don't even know where she is?

The days pass. My memories of Chana grow more vivid. I'm remembering everything — the ghetto, jail, Auschwitz — and yet I still have one question I cannot answer: Is Chana real or just someone my guilty conscience has created?

She has to exist, I tell myself.

I pray for courage. I pray that when the time comes for me to speak, for me to tell the story, I'll know what to say.

———

I want to go home, I'm ready. I want to speak to Simon. He's already home. I want to tell him I understand and ask him to understand me. I'm afraid of what he will say, of what's going to happen to me. I'm afraid of what I have to do.

I ask Mama if she's sure there has been no one, besides her, staying with me in the hospital room while I was in the coma.

"No, no one else," she says. "Now come on, let's see how you sit in your wheelchair."

I know she's worried about me. I know she doesn't like my questions. She has sensed the sadness growing in me as the days pass and I remember more of this other life, my life as Chana.

I try to joke with her. "This is ridiculous. I don't need a wheelchair. I'm a pro with these crutches." I whirl around on one foot.

"Hey now, watch out. If you trip while on your way out of the hospital, you could end up back in bed, so just get in the chair, Hilly. Just do it."

"Yes, Mama." I hobble over to the chair and fall back into it.

"Such grace."

"Of course. I trained with the Royal Ballet."

"More like the Royal Air Force."

"Very funny, haha."

"Excuse me. I'm sorry to interrupt, but are you Hilary Burke?" A woman wearing a blue hat and coat and looking strangely familiar stands in the doorway.

"Yes, I'm Hilary." I wheel around to face her.

"I know this is a bit unusual. I'm Nadia Bergman. My sister was in the intensive care unit with you." She looks at my mother. "Perhaps you remember seeing me, Mrs. Burke."

"No, I'm sorry, I . . ."

"You're Nadzia! You're Chana's baby sister!" I say.

"Thank goodness you know me. I didn't know how I was going to explain myself. Maybe Chana knew what she was talking about after all."

"Chana? Is she here?"

"Hilary, who is Chana? I'm afraid, Mrs. Bergman, I don't understand."

"I don't understand much myself. My sister told me to give this to you, Hilary. She died. Of cancer."

"Yes, she — I remember — I mean, I'm sorry, too." I look down at the book she has placed in my lap.

"This is — it's the photo album!"

"Hilary, I've never seen that book in all my life. Who are all those people?"

"They're my family, Mrs. Burke."

"Then why are you giving this to Hilary? This is crazy."

"I have saved some, but I never knew any of them — except Chana. I was sent away from them when I was just an infant. They all died in the war. Chana was the only survivor. She came to the States to live near me. I'm sorry, I don't really understand myself, but it is Chana's last request that Hilary have it."

"No — Hilary, we must give the book back, don't you think? How could these people have anything to do with you?"

"I'm sorry to upset you. Chana said Hilary would understand."

"Hilary?"

"Yes, I understand. I remember." I look back up at Nadzia. "There's this notation in the front of the book — Jeremiah 1: 4-10."

"Yes, Chana told me to put that there. Again, she said you would understand."

"Well, Mama, you have your Bible. What does it say?"

"Oh — okay, let me see now." She fumbles with the book. "Yes, here we go . . .

"Now the word of the Lord came to me saying,
'Before I formed you in the womb I knew you,
and before you were born I consecrated you;
I appointed you a prophet to the nations.'
Then I said, 'Ah Lord God! Behold,
I do not know how to speak,
for I am only a youth.'
But the Lord said to me,
'Do not say, "I am only a youth;"
for to all to whom I send you you shall go,
and whatever I command you you shall speak.
Be not afraid of them,
For I am with you to deliver you,'
says the Lord.
Then the Lord put forth his hand
and touched my mouth; and the Lord said to me,
'Behold, I have put my words in your mouth.
See, I have set you this day over nations and over kingdoms,
to pluck up and to break down,
to destroy and to overthrow,
to build and to plant.' "